let me tell you

and **let me go on**

PAUL GRIFFITHS

 **New York Review Books** New York

This is a New York Review Book

published by The New York Review of Books

207 East 32nd Street, New York, NY 10016

www.nyrb.com

Copyright © 2008, 2023 by Paul Griffiths
All rights reserved.

let me tell you first published in 2008 by Reality Street and republished in 2023 by Henningham Family Press; *let me go on* first published in 2023 by Henningham Family Press

Library of Congress Cataloging-in-Publication Data
Names: Griffiths, Paul, 1947 November 24– author. | Griffiths, Paul, 1947 November 24– Let me tell you. | Griffiths, Paul, 1947 November 24– Let me go on.
Title: Let me tell you ; and Let me go on / by Paul Griffiths.
Other titles: Let me go on
Description: New York : New York Review Books, 2025. | Series: New York Review Books |
Identifiers: LCCN 2024052311 (print) | LCCN 2024052312 (ebook) | ISBN 9781681379258 (paperback) | ISBN 9781681379265 (ebook)
Subjects: LCSH: Ophelia (Fictitious character)—Fiction. | LCGFT: Novels.
Classification: LCC PR6057.R515 L48 2025 (print) | LCC PR6057.R515 (ebook) | DDC 823/.914—dc23/eng/20241115
LC record available at https://lccn.loc.gov/2024052311
LC ebook record available at https://lccn.loc.gov/202

ISBN 978-1-68137-925-8
Available as an electronic book; 978-1-68137-926-5

The authorized representative in the EU for product safety and compliance is eucomply OÜ, Pärnu mnt 139b-14, 11317 Tallinn, Estonia, hello@eucompliancepartner.com, +33 757690241.

Printed in the United States of America on acid-free paper
10 9 8 7 6 5 4 3 2 1

Contents

for Anne

* * * * * *

let me tell you

Read Me

I do not know, now, how all this will end. You will see, in what follows, what Ophelia will have to say of her life before the start of our play. You will hear her speak of her father, Polonius, and of her brother, Laertes. They were with us all the time, so you will hear her speak of me, of my wife, Gertrude, and of the son Gertrude had with my brother: Hamlet. And all this Ophelia will speak in her own words, those words alone. She is like the rest of us; we all have no more than the words that come to us in the play. We go on with these words. We have to. But if we should break them up, as Ophelia does here, what then? And look: I too have gone from my part. I begin to fear. I have loved my life as it is, say what you will.

— *The King*

1

So: now I come to speak. At last. I will tell you all I know. I was deceived to think I could not do this. I have the powers; I take them here. I have the right. I have the means. My words may be poor, but they will have to do.

What words do I have? Where do they come from? How is it that I speak?

There will be a time for me to think of these things, but right now I have to tell you all that I may of me—of me from when I lay on my father's knees and held up my hand, touching his face, which he had bended down over me. That look in his eyes....

My father.

Well, I have done what I could. And I believe, by now, I have done *all* that I could. That's the reason there's this difference in me now, that I may speak my thoughts as I wish.

Still, it's hard. I see that face of his. What would he wish me to do?

That face. What does it say?

There may be some will tell me I cannot remember from being so little, and they may be right. Some of these may be false remembrances, things my father would say to me, and say again, time upon time, as was his way, so that I think I remember them. I must do all I may to find from them what is truly mine, now that I have made up my mind to speak to you like this.

There are so many of these things. It's as if I held a glass in my hand and could see them all, there in the glass, the things I remember, remembrances all tumbled one upon another, some before they should be, some late, all out of time—the sun over the cold green mountain, a scholar with a hard look in his eyes, my father shaking as he rose to give a speech, my brother with flowers in his hand and he would not say what for, a lost sandal, a music lesson—and it's up to me to be patient and lay them down the right way.

There are things, as well, I do not see, things that come to me as speech, and some as music. A call.

'O, please come now! Now!'

Is this my father? No.

'O, how long must I be down here without you?'

I see the young me, up the cold green mountain, down on the grass, one hand on—what is it?—some little herb. And still that call. She cannot let me be.

'O, come now! Right away! You should be here with me!'

I lay still. It's as if I was held by what was in my hand, by what my hand was touching. It's as if I had been locked there, locked to the mountain, with my eyes quite still, on my hand and the herb in the grass. And all the powers in hell could not have made me go from there.

But I, such a little nothing as I was, I could make me go—did make me go.

'O, *now!* Do you—?'

She—this young me—I see look up, but not at these words. My arm rises to keep my eyes from the sun. I see it. This is indeed as it was. I remember. An arm rises to the sun, a head from what thoughts it had, two knees from the grass. There was that call, but it seemed to come from a long way away, whilst in my head was another call, no words this time—the call of my thoughts. What should I do? Which path should I take? This way, that way?

'O, please, you cannot go away by yourself!'

I look at me now as I was then. This is like being one of my own observers, but with no powers over what is observed. It all must go as it does. All I may do is see what this little I will do. I look in the glass to do so: I raised my head. My hand let go the herb. I have gone, down the mountain. I have gone.

What was I then? Two? Two up the mountain, two as this little I goes down the mountain with a good grace, as she answers the call that had come?

Let time be turned from here. Let these little treads I make down the mountain go up again, restore that right hand to the herb it held, that head to the patient perusal it made. Let little I be there again in the grass, and from here go on and on to before all this, to where she—I—had come from.

This is it. Let me go right away, now, whilst it is still not late, to before all this—to before the mountain and the unbraced out-doors and the little me in it all, with my hand touching the herb and my head in the heavens, to before the time these eyes of mine look up, as I see them look up now, to before that last call to come in.

'O, that's right! Come here. Down to me. See what I have for you.'

Do not fear: that's what I would say to this little me now. The time will come when you do not have to go down there, when you do not have to do what she will ask, when you may please yourself.

This is it, now, that time. It's come.

So let's go on to before, all the way to the end of my memory, to what was for me Day One. Let's come to that day she bore me, the day I draw breath.

It's like this. It is morning. The sun is pale; it's a cold morning.

There she is, on the bed. She does not look at the window, to the sun, but away, to the door, as if in expectation that some one would come in. I see all this, for some reason, as if from by the window.

There's another one there. Right. My father. The pale morning sun stole from the window over the bed and over the bed clothes, and now it falls in my memory on them: she on the bed, my father, and no doubt another they would have had there to be a help.

He—my father—could never keep still. He comes and goes from one end of the chamber to the other—one way, then the other, his eyes down. And she, she does not look at him but still at the door, never but at the door. They do not speak. There is no more than this: his treads on the stone, up and down.

But let all this go, for how could I remember this day? How could I remember a time when I was not?

I have to think more before I go on like this. False memory may speak, I find, as well as true. I have to know the difference. And I have to see to it that I do not make things up. It's hard. Indeed, it may well seem hard for all of us, to know what it is that we truly know—and what it is that we know to be true. Another difference, it may be. There is more in my mind than I know. I must look hard at what comes to me, cast away the grass and keep the flowers.

I know I have it in me to say things that are not so and have never been so, but that I wish had been so. There are, as well, things in my head that I cannot remember and never will remember. They are not in my memory; they are in me.

But now and again words come to me as if it

rained words in my head—words given me by some other, as if I had no hand in what I say, as if all I may do is give speech, let the words come and come, and go on and on, and whilst they go on I cannot say what I would truly wish to say. I may do nothing, held still by my own words—if they are my own. My words go on, but *I* cannot speak.

I have to make it so that my face cannot speak without my mind, that my words do not take form other than as I wish.

I will do so. Mark my words.

So on with it. That mountain: it was a green sandal loosed from the heels of heaven.

I remember it well. My hand touching that herb. A shirt, held out of a window, shaking in the morning sun. The way the maid's head was raised as if to sing, but then she goes on with the sewing. And over all the cold green mountain.

Each morning the sun would come up over the mountain, and we would pray, my father and I, and then with my brother as well, pray for a good day, and pray at the end of the day for a good night.

This was when *she* had gone. She left when I was little, but that's one of the things I'll come to.

If things still come out of my jangled memory here and there before they should, that could be for woe, but then again it could be for joy—if not for the two, hand in hand. But I will do all I may to have things right from here on.

The day I have to find in my memory now is another day, and a day of joy this one was, the day when I was given my brother.

This is something I do indeed remember—and this is where that false memory comes from, of the one on the bed, and the pale morning sun, and the bed clothes, and the head turned away, and my father as he made his way up and down.

I would have been still little when she bore him, but more than I was in that other memory, of being up the mountain.

As I remember, hard as this may be to believe, I was there, there on the bed, my little hand touching that face. She and I. (This is not something I like to remember at all. That means it must be true.)

And no, my father was not there. There must have been other treads of his that go on in my mind.

My father was not with us for some reason. It could be that he had to be with His Majesty that morning, for—and no doubt it would have been better to say this before—he was one of the king's right-hand men. He was at the king's call, day and night. He is now, he is still. Do this, do that.

But no, it's not quite like that. My father is the king's shoulder: that's how it is. The two of them know each other so well that my father does not have to think what the king will say. Indeed, he could almost speak for the king, and the day may come when he will have to, if the king's not better before long.

So it was with the king as was, at the time I now speak of, that my father was held in honour and had to go all over for him. Then we, my brother and I, would have to do without him whilst he was away. She, at such a time, was the one we had to go to.

But again I go on before I should. I'll come to all this, of my father, and the counsel he would give the king—the king as was and the king we have now. This will all come out at the right time.

As for now, there we are, on the bed in the pale morning: she and me. That's what I remember. That's how it was.

No, that's still not right, cannot be. There was another. I have it. The maid. The maid's here with us as well, by the bed. How could I not remember that the maid was there?

And then there he was: my brother. The maid

took him up by the heels. I see this. To me he had a puffed-up look—'bonny', the maid would say. He sucked in one breath, and with that my love, little as I was. He did not weep, not at all, but let out something like a little moan, as if—so it seemed to me—he could say 'O'. And he turned his eyes to look at me.

So now there are two of us. That's good. It was good not to be by yourself with such a one as she was. We had each other now. My brother and I had each other.

The maid held him—my brother—close with one hand before she had to lay him down on the bed. There I could look and look at him.

Then she took him away again, to redeliver him to us in a long shirt (the one they would christen him in). Now he was right by me. I remember a little ankle, remember touching a little ankle. I remember touching his face with my tongue.

He was still. All was still. All is still.

And out of that still morning I seem to remember how the maid would sing to us. Was it then? Most of the time she would sing to us at night, as she took us to bed.

There was a lady all in green,
Nony the nony no no,
Was locked away and was not seen,
Nony the nony no no.
Quoth she: 'I cannot find my tear,
The tear that falls each morning here,
The tear of grace, the tear of fear,
The tear that falls upon the bier',
Nony the nony no no.

A young lord by the window stayed,
Nony the nony no no,
And bended to this speech she made,
Nony the nony no no.
He left that day to find the tear,
The tear of grace, the tear of fear,
The tear that falls each morning here,
The tear that falls upon the bier,
Nony the nony no no.

He did not look down to the grass,
Nony the nony no no,
He did not see the rose of glass,
Nony the nony no no.
The rose of grace, the rose of fear,
The rose that falls each morning here,
The rose of glass that was the tear,

The rose that falls upon the bier,
Nony the nony no no.

There's more I have to say of the maid—more I would wish to say of the maid—and let me say it now here, all of it.

She was not young. But to a little one that means nothing. What meant all to us was that, without being quite one of us, she was with us. If there was one lesson we took from the maid, it was to know what you are—to know what you are in yourself, and all you may be. She did not take a command well, not from me and not from my brother. Never. But if you would ask, there was nothing she would not do for you.

She honoured my father.

What she may have been like to the other when no-one was there with them, I do not know.

To us two, my brother and I.... Well, she blasted us with love, day upon day.

She held us, one in each arm, and held us to each other. She would look down at us and say nothing—say nothing but look and look, harsh with love.

I remember that breath on my face. I remember that look: harsh indeed, but sweet as well. And the more I think of it, what I remember most of all is a long-lost perfume: the perfume of being held, of clothes on my face.

This is the maid, in my memory, as she was, the one that held us. She comes from some way away, from over the mountain. She does what she must, and more. Nothing does she say, not to us, most of the time. But we look as she goes from one chamber to another. We do not know if she'll mind that she's being observed: we are young and do not think of that. And if she does know we are there, she does not let on. We go where she goes. We, that know what it is to be patient observers, look on as she does what she does.

She would go to the well each morning. I see a hard cold hand.

On the day when the baker would come to the door, she would ask us what we would wish for—'wish for', she would say. Ask us, not my father, and not the other.

We would go to see them at the door, my brother and I. We would look at them, the maid and the baker, for as long as they stayed there. We could not tell, from where we lay, what these two would say to each other. But we could see. There would be a difference in the maid's face.

Other things.

She did not blame us when it rained and a glass of pansies (I think) by the window—indeed, pansies they must have been, from by the path—was blown over.

She took us out one night to see an owl. My father did not know of this. She did not tell us what we would see, but raised a hand to show us the owl, pale in the night like a saint.

When she *did* speak, it was in the way of over the mountain. 'See' would be more like 'say', and 'say' like 'sigh'. 'Fair' and 'fare' would be more like 'fear'. There was, as well, something hard in this breath-cast speech. It was as if she did not wish to speak, longed never to speak at all, and so words —when indeed words would come—would have to come out all at one go.

One day we, my brother and me, made it seem we had lost all powers of speech and would have to speak by means of letters. (When you are little you do these things.) I remember how, at the table, with my brother close by, I held that hard cold hand to help the maid form some words. Little madam that I was!

But the 'A' she made was more like an 'S', and my brother had to say 'No, that's not it at all', and right away she was up from the table, and the lesson had come to an end.

That look as she left: I see it now.

She was no beauty, not at all, but to me she was beauteous—to me and to my brother. Beauteous: it's one of the words that, to me, goes with the maid and no other. And beauteous she must have been to the baker, for there comes the day when she goes away with him, over the mountain again. She did not tell us she was to go. Did she think that, had she done so, she could have been stayed by us, held there by us? We go down one morning to find she's gone. That was that.

It was a late love for the two of them. It was a love we had observed but not seen. It was a love that was for them, for the two of them, of each for the other, not for us to know.

As I think of the maid, the remembrances come one upon another: a look that could say more than words, a hand on my arm. And this: the grace that made, I will now say, a home.

2

Let me come to another day—another day that is not like this one now, where time goes on, and I have to say what I may whilst I still may do so, for I do not know what time I have.

But there, in my memory, time is still.

Here, here as I speak, I know what it is to be me: to be one, on my own. There I have to find this other me, the one I was—which means there are two: me now and me then. Indeed, there may be more: a chorus of me, the observed and the observers. Here the day may go as it will—and all I may do is hope it will go well. There, there in the glass, it is done. It's all over.

No, it's not over as long as I have not done with it. It's stayed. There may be more to it than I have seen. Many things have stayed in that way: the day I lost my way up the mountain when I turned from the path; the day I promised my father I would see to some form for him and then did not do it—so many things that it's hard for me to know which should come before another.

And then there are the things I would see time and again, so that they seem in my memory to make up one day—one day that turned like a wheel.

Is this no more than the effect of memory, that one day will seem like another? No, for the young this is how it is. Time then did not go on. All was before you, still to come. No one left. Nothing was lost for good. And what was death?

Each morning I see the maid on the way to the well.

Each morning my brother rises from his little bed and comes to me in mine.

Each morning what my brother and I have to say to each other, him and then me, is what's come to us in the night. A king with a withered arm. Another king with one good daughter and two that are not. The table turned on an ungartered steward.

Each morning we have to be patient—but never with each other. No, being with each other was not hard. We had to be patient before the time when my father could see us. So we stayed in bed. Then my father would come to the door.

Each morning, in bed, the words tumbled on and on as we tumbled over each other, and then more as we lay quite still.

'I was up the mountain and there was a bed of flowers by the path, you know. There was a rose with the face of a lady, but she did not speak. I could see long columbines with eyes all their length, but I do not think they could see me. And some pansies, like there are. I had gone to take one up and, touching it, it made me cold all over, and I took a look down at my hand, and it had turned my hand green.'

I see this now as I could see it then. I look as my hand becomes a dove, a green dove, and is loosed from my arm, and goes up and away. And then I look again, and my hand is as it was.

'Are they all down on the ground?'

'What?'

'The flowers.'

'No.'

'So what made you say they lay in bed?'

Then each morning we would go down to be with them—my father and *she* and the maid: two at the table, with us two, whilst the maid does things for us.

Each morning we have to see what we have seen before—each morning, that is, before the day *she* left.

If my father was not there, the maid would call us down, and it would be us and the other one at the table. The maid would come to us with a glass in each hand—one for my brother, one for me—and say nothing. The other one would say nothing. So it would go on. The maid, with nothing now to do, would go to the window and look out at the mountain.

When my father is there and the two of them are at the table, they say 'Good morning' as we come in, and we say 'Good morning' as well. That's all. Then, as the maid does what she must, *she*, the other one, goes on with that way she had, that perusal of my father, and he goes on as if there's nothing to it. When all's done we go out.

We go out. My brother was two by now, and I held him by the hand as we took the path up the mountain—right up to the brow, for it seemed to us we had to go all the way up before we could play.

It was not that we did not wish for them to know what we did. By no means. There was nothing of that in it. But we had to be away. That was all.

At the brow of the mountain we stayed, and did not go down before the morning was quite over.

It's all here, in my mind, right as it was. I could be lost in it, and not come away. But I will.

He was sweet in his sun hat.

We stayed, as I say, at the brow of the mountain. There we are.

I look at him. He had a hand raised over his eyes.

He does not know what I will do. How could he? I did not know. And I did not know at the time what made me do what I did. But I think I know now. We had come from that table, from the two that had nothing to say to each other.

I took my right arm. I sucked and sucked at it.

He made a little moan, as before. It turned out to be a way he had when there was something he could not do with.

But I had to go on: there was something I had to show him. I did not know what, but there was something I had to show him, here and now.

It does not go right. I see him weep. Tear on tear falls hard from his eyes. The mountain grass was bewept.

My arm falls and I draw to him a little, but without quite touching. I do not know what to do.

There we are, not quite touching. My hand is not quite on his shoulder. But still, his little weep and his moan are over. His eyes are on me, as they had been before, all the time.

Then I show him my arm. There is a mark on my arm. It rises as we look.

And there is the sun, and there is the mountain: all where we are is in an ecstasy of expectation.

We look at the mark on my arm—his eyes and mine, on that mark. Then we look at each other. There is nothing to say.

I see us go down again, hand in hand.

It's not like that now. Now he's away on his own, my brother, his hand, I know, in another's. And that's good. That's as it should be.

But it must be from him, from being with him, that I have come to know how good, how right, it is to find a hand in mine, not locked but loosed there, touching. There's a difference now, as I do not have to say. Still, here on the brow of the mountain, with my little brother, this is, I believe, where I find what it's like to have a hand in my own, find how it would please me—the joy it would give me to know that some other is truly there, with me, as close as a hand's touching.

A hand is affection. A hand is honour. A hand is honesty.

A hand is mercy, the hand of one to another, a hand to help.

It is holy, the touching of a hand.

A hand given is one of the gifts of the heart.

A hand may say this: 'I will be with you, from now to the end of time. I will never let you go. You will think of me as your own. I will be your own.'

A hand may be an argument to them that do not believe in love.

'Here is my hand', one will say. 'This is my hand. I give you my hand.' There's nothing I may give you that means more.

'I take your hand', the other will say. 'I have your hand in mine.' There's nothing I may take from you that means more. 'And in being like that, I have given you my hand. This is my hand. This is me.'

Here: I have held it out to you. Take my hand. Go with me. Be with me.

Not all remembrances are good to restore to the mind. I'll come again to my brother and me on the mountain, how we would go there in the sun to play. But for now let me go on.

Months have gone by from the morning of the mark on my arm. No-one other than us, my brother and I, had given it a look—no, not the maid. I did not like to keep things from the maid, but this time I had to, so it seemed to me. And my brother, so young, could say nothing of what had gone on. That was a help, in a way. In another way it was not. The shame was more.

Morning upon morning, when in bed with me, he had come and held my arm to his face, touching where the mark was to his face. That was all. He would have it so, my arm held to his face, his little hand on it as we lay there. Nothing did we say to one another. And we could see the mark go down.

Then there had to come the time when they would not let us play all day long. Before we could go out we had to do the morning's lesson, which would be in commerce, letters, music and so on.

Two men would come each morning to give us the lesson of the day. One of them had a way of touching his tongue with his hand when he had to think. The other was pale and grave of feature, and had the look of a courtier that had been denied something.

They do not come now—indeed, they have

not come for a long time—but they are still here close by, and I see them now and then. They do not seem to know me. They go by without a look.

I cannot say I mind: I could never find a way to like them. But still, they are good men. And over the months we had with them—months and months, lesson upon lesson—they did what they had come to do. I have to say that. There we would all be, day in, day out, and they would speak to us, of this, that and the other. Most of the time we would say nothing: there was no expectation that we would. They did not ask for my thoughts, and they did not ask for my brother's. But we would find we had come to know things we did not know before.

Not all of these things have stayed with me. Indeed, I wish I could remember more from that morning lesson we would have each day. As it is, what's left to me is a little here and there—things it would be hard to call 'memory'.

But let me see what I may call to mind.

Naught, one, two, and so on. Naught. How I would find it hard to believe in that naught! Still do. Nothing. But nothing as something, something you call naught. So not nothing at all. There is no nothing. Nothing is something. Naught. O.

And music. Let me say here all that I know of music: it will not take long.

The late king composed—the king that died by his own hand, as some say, but that's another of the things I'll come to. Indeed he did, composed —with no other to help him—things he had some of us do each Valentine's Day as a charity show: I was in more than one of them. *The Honourable Libertine, Other Pastors, Tenders Tomorrow, Never Love a Scholar*—and all with his own words, musicked by himself. He was quite something—in what he would go for, one must say. I was not that keen on most of his music; still, I could not but see what it meant to him.

And he composed chamber music as well. There was a tune in the key of A—the key of love, I believe. Now, that was something that's stayed in my mind. It was a tune my father would like to play, and I would ask him to play it again, and he would make as if to do so, his hand raised, but he could never play it twice, it made him weep so. That was the effect on him. To me it seemed sweet, that tune. To him there was more to it. I never could find out quite what. But then, I did not ask.

More of these things come to me. *Beauty's*

Argument, The Two Noble Watchmen, Better Believe It! This last was poor, to my mind. But I was on my own in that: it was held to be good by most observers, I have to say, and for some it was right at the head of the king's music. They remember it still. Better believe it.

There's something in one of these things of the king's: I cannot remember which, but it was not that one, I know. It's a tune that's almost like 'Remember Me', but not quite. The chorus goes like this:

O, but no. I cannot sing. I cannot sing, not now. That time is over and done with. Music died here: it died when the late king died. It is no more. It's gone for good.

If you wish to have music, you must tear yourself away and go from here. Here all is still, still as night. We do not have the joy of music.

It's as if a robin rises and there's nothing. It's as if a glass falls and there's nothing. That's the way of it.

There was a time when I could sing, and then I would sing and sing. My father would love to have me sing to him, at the end of a hard day. But that's all over. Now he would say, if one should ask, that he's no time for music. And what is music if not time: time of now and then tumbled in to one another, time turned and loosed, time sweet and harsh, flowers of time?

But to go on with what I still know of the music that was here of late, no other but the king composed for us. His was all the music we had, such as it was.

I know I must seem to say little of his stature, but he left us all, I think, with the wish that we could have had other music, if no more than for the difference of it. Difference is good: each becomes better than it was, if there's some play of one with another. So, whilst I did, come to think, quite like some of the king's things, I would wish there had been other music. Now I wish there could be *some* music.

There was a time when I would play as well as sing, and play quite well, I think. But it never seemed to me I could have composed. Music was something given.

Then music was something given *up*. But no, it was more as if music had given us up.

Me-la-so, I seem to remember—remember, it would seem, from so long a time—, *la-so-me*. But what this means to me now is no more than words, little words, and words without a tune.

It's like this. These of us that are still here—and I think I may speak for all of us in this—have lost the affection we had for music. That's hard. Without affection music means nothing. It is cold thoughts and form. It is snow on your grave. It is a soldier that treads on the snow on your grave. One, two. One, two. One, two.

That's all I know of music. That's all I remember of music.

My brother could play better than I could—and sing as well, but it was hard to make him. Still, there was one lesson where I was better than him by a long way, which was when we had to speak in another tongue.

I would give him what help I could. '*Do-no*' I would say, to show the right length of each 'o'. I give. You, my brother, give. He, my master, will give. She is given. We are the givers. They should have had the gifts. These could not have been the gifts that should have been given.

Now and again my father would help us in this when he had been away for the king. So did my father's brother one time. He, like my father, was on the king's staff.

He was a good soul, so like my father in many things. I say 'was', for he is no more with us, alas: he died a little before the late king, and on that day (I see it now), as we lay him in the ground up there, the sun comes out, and it would seem the mountain rises a little to close over him. I remember how he held us, my brother and me, one on each of his knees, as he would tell us what he had seen whilst he was away. And we would be touching his beard. My father did not have a beard at that time, so his brother's beard—which was like snow—was something I could not take my eyes away from. So it was with my little brother. There we would be, each of us with a hand in it. You would think that would have made it hard for him to speak, but he let us be. And we would look at him, look at his beard, see it shaking a little with his breath—the breath that was on my brother's hand as it was on mine.

There was a time he had come over-night from Givers-la-Rède, and took us on his knees to say this:

'My my, I think they are all pansies over there, you know. Nothing means more to them than fashion. I took the coach to where the Sun King made his home. Chamber upon chamber upon chamber, all with glass doors. Quite good. But no baker there could make what we have at home. Nothing like.'

And here I could see him look at the maid. But she stayed bended down sewing, as if she would give him no mind. That was how they had been with each other from long before. How could she speak from the heart when this was the master's brother? And he, how could he show his hand?

My father was there this time, the other not. That would be the way of it.

'I had to have many a lesson in how they speak,' he goes on, 'before I could go and whilst I was there as well. Would you like me to tell you something of it?'

And how could we say no?

'*Non* means *no*.'

I think: My brother, little as he is, does not find these things so hard he could not have done that one for himself. I look over at him. He, like me, still had his hand in that snow-beard, and he does not look my way. I say nothing. No more does he. We are of one mind on that. No one could be unkind to Gis.

Then, with the beard now still, we see that the time's come for one of us to say something, ask something. I look at my brother again. He's shaking his head a little. Then I speak.

'What's the most you may say then, Gis?'

At this good Gis stayed down in his thoughts a

little—down, but with his eyes up to think.

'Well, my little two,'—he would call us this, his 'little two'—'I'll give this a go. Let's see how many words I may remember if I think hard. Right.'

Then he turned to look at us, from one to the other.

'La rue Saint-Valentine, long, a if à but; la rose pâle me face à la table.'

'Good heavens, that's something', I say: no doubt this would have come from my father's way of speech. 'Let's have it again.'

'La rue Saint-Valentine, long, a if à but; la rose pâle me face à la table. O la la, o la la.'

So it goes, this time with a little tune at the end.

That means it's over to me again. What shall I say? Then it comes to me: ask him if he had another tongue he could speak in.

Gis cast his eyes down. Did I know there was something not quite right here? Did I know what this would have raised up in his mind?

I believe not. There would be another day, another time, when Gis would tell us of the time when he was a soldier a long way from home, how he had held one of his men as he died, and 'they did not tell us how to lay out the dead'.

As for now, he let us down from his knees. Was

it over? I took a look at him, then at my brother, with his eyes still on Gis. I held out my hand, which my brother took, but he could not let go of Gis with his eyes. I turned away a little, to draw him with me, and as he turned as well, Gis took us again with his words.

'*O arm' Held in See*'—the way he does this is with me still: it's like music, as if he would speak and sing at the one time—

> *O arm' Held in See,*
> *So hat hell' Bier in Hand,*
> *So is't all's Form an End.*

I look at him: there's a tear in his eye, and his mind must be with this '*arm' Held*'—this poor soldier, as I was to find out, this soldier all on his own, his day long over, but this soldier that still stayed where he was, and did not close his eyes to the night of nothing.

3

Now and again the maid would go away, over the mountain, to see the daughter she had—the daughter that was all this time with the maid's brother. (This was before the maid left to go away for good with the baker, at which time he took the daughter as his own.) As I remember, she would go for the night and be with us again late in the morning. Then she would let some months go by before she would go again.

As a little one I did not like it when she was gone. When I rose in the morning there would be something I could not quite remember—did not wish to remember. Then I would. And I fear I took it out on my brother. I did not wish to have him come in then, and he would know that. He did not ask me to play. I would go down without him to the door, which had a window in it. And there, for as long as the maid was gone, I stayed to see when she would come down the mountain again to be with us. Then at last, when I could see the maid, I would be up and away.

'The maid is here, the maid is here', I would say over and over, like a little tune, as I made my way up the mountain, up to the maid, so that we could come down again hand in hand.

There must have been many a time like that. This was one: I had seen the maid come over the brow of the mountain and had gone out, my head raised and my heart with it.

It was a harsh cold day. On the turf to the right of the path, all the flowers had been blown down, and there was no sun. But I did not mind.

'The maid is here, the maid is here. The maid is here, the maid is here.'

So I come now to the maid on the path, and she comes to me, one arm held out, whilst in the other she had the things she took.

I take that hand I know so well in mine and we look at each other as she comes down close to me. She does not have to ask how things have been.

We stayed there, on and on, with me held by that arm on my shoulder, and she bended over to me, as if we did not wish to go home. For me this was home, to be with the maid, for as long as she held me. This—I say it again—was what made home. This and my brother. But with my brother, it was more that I made a home for him. That was what the maid did for me. My father could not: he had his own things to do, and he would go away for months at a time, so that I could not think of him that way. The heart of what made a home was the maid. There was no door we had to go in. Home could be out on the mountain—out on the blown grass, as it was here, when I was held by the maid.

I draw away a little, and the maid's hand falls from me.

'Did you find your daughter in good form?' I ask, as I look away. My hope is to say something that means little, but I know right away the words have not come out right. They never do, with the maid and me. It's better if we do not speak, for all that we have to say may be done without words. Words are in the way. And these words of mine come out as if she and I had not been close at all.

The maid's are no better. The effect they make is indeed of a maid, of one that must do and be what the master's daughter will ask. This is not how it is with us. But we cannot find the words for what we are.

'Ay, she's quite t' young lady now, my love, gramercy. All she will think of, would you believe, is fashion, from morning to night. There was a feature in one of them Sundays on Christ-ian.... Nay, I cannot remember on Christian what. Christian this, Christian that: there are so many Christians. And these things never meant no-thing to me, I have to say. But she...!'

'Clothes?' I say. 'What does she like? You must take some of mine to your daughter, by all means, please. I have so many.'

And indeed I had. *She* let me have all I could wish for. In all honesty I have to say she did that for me.

There may have been something in this I could not see: it may not have been done for me` at all. In all she did there would be some other reason. Nothing was as it seemed.

My clothes. I remember a shirt with bells on the right arm; a pale green stole dupped with columbines; stockings, stockings, stockings, in my closet and all over my chamber; a doublet made for me, of wax may-flowers and owl down, which I donned for a play; a long sandal—one long sandal, for I had lost the other one.

'Nay, my love,'—for so she would call me, most of all when she had been away—'give o'er. You are good, but oh... (a long breath) I would not wish this daughter of mine more puffed-up than 'a' is. Keep what th'hadst. Belike she'll then come to know what she is and what she comes from. That'll be hard, I know, but she must.'

That was all she would say. End of speech. If I should ask again what I could find for that daughter, she would say nothing to me. I know that. She never answers again when she's had to say no, so I give up.

Did she, another day, say more of this daughter? I cannot remember so well, but no, I think not. And there had still been nothing more by the day she took me (my brother was not with us) over the mountain to where the daughter was.

Over the mountain we have gone, without two words to say, all morning long. That's how it should be: we are on the right path with each other now.

Before we left she did, I remember, ask me if I would like to go. 'Will you come with me this time?' That was all she had to say. 'Indeed I will.' She had my things, for she would know she had but to ask. So we left.

And there: from up over the brow of the mountain we could see it. We had turned, and there it was, quite close down there, where the maid's brother's tumbled-down little home was.

I see the maid now. She treads down the steep path, and so do I, down to the door. She goes before me. We go one by one, in tune with each other.

Late that night, when I was in bed, in a chamber all my own, I lay with my eyes on the door.

At home the maid would come in each night to see that I was all right, but on this night, with a brother and a daughter to keep in mind, she was late. And she did not seem so composed. She had a deject look, as if there was something she had to tell me but did not wish to.

She stayed by the door. I think she will speak from there, but then she comes over to my bed. When I was little and had a cold she would come in bed with me. This she does not do now, but, bended down, with a hand on my arm, she is there by me, still with that look. Then out it comes, this long speech she seemed to know by heart, almost as if she had done it before, and that goes on and on, words she had to tell me. I remember it all: when she did it, how she did it, and what she had to say.

As to the how, she did not speak this time the way she did most of the time, the over-the-mountain way, but more like us. I did not think of this right then, but it could be she had been given this long speech by my father. I could see this, the two of them in his morning chamber, where she would have to say it over and over to him, like a lesson, so he would know she had it right. But if so, what reason could he have had not to tell me all this himself? I cannot think.

As to the what, here it is:

'Words are what he will say.

' "Words" is what he will say.

' "Words, words, words."

'He'll say this to your father, when the two of them are with each other, and—as he must think —no other is there with them. Never for a breath must he know that the king is close by as well, out of the way.

'What more do we know of him? That he's a scholar. That his shirt is like night. That he's a little ungracious now and then. Do I have to say more? That his father was—at the time we speak of—the king of Denmark. Now do you know him? That his father's brother is the king of Denmark. (Indeed it is so. This is the way it will have turned out.) That you will have seen him, over the months of death and joy there will have been by then—for all this will come—, worse than he was and better than he will be. That in his face there's something of his soul—something of such cold woe that one could weep. That he is, as we speak, not one of the dead. Death will come to him, as to us all—as to, I should say, many of us. Not all. Not quite all.'

This I have had come to mind again and again. I know that what she had to say to me here was a way to counsel me, if I could but make it out. But there are many things that I never have made out—and this last most of all. For death cannot be deceived. Death comes not to 'many of us' but indeed to all—if not, then there will have to be an end before death.

I think of what this other end could be, the end that is not death, the end that is before death, the end that may, then, have loosed us from death, should we have that grace.

The end, the end.

The more I think of these words of the maid's, the more I wish she had had more to say that night. At the time I did not think to ask for more: it did not seem it was mine to ask, but to receive. But I ask now.

Which of us will not have to see death? What becomes of them that have not died at the end? What, indeed, is the end if not death? Where may we go other than to flowers and the bier, with pastors to pray for us, bewept by all and by bells?

You see, my own words give me reason for doubt. I have these words that keep thoughts of death in my mind, an expectancy I cannot repel, but which rises up again and again, and I have to draw hard away from it.

No more of that. Please.

It is as if my own words could tell me, before the time, of my death. This is the reason I think there will not be an end for me that is not death. This is the reason I believe I will be one of the dead, one of the died and gone, like grass, when the end comes. So I do not have to mind what that other end will be. It will not come for me. There will be no end but death, death that comes in pale clothes.

No.

I say no to death. But what is my 'no' to this pale being that will come to take me with him? Will he let me go?

I hope my father will not see death. I hope he will go on to find that other end—as it would be, over the mountain of death, if not before that mountain. And my brother. I wish I could know this, could find it out from their words.

Please, no more.

If the maid is right, they will be dead before the end. I wish I could say no for them as well, for all that my own words seem to speak of death.

But do I long for death and not know it? Is that what my words tell me? I think of something Gis would sing, when we had music, something that's stayed with me all this time, from Gis with his beard of snow.

All will come to their own last breath,
Lady, lord and scholar.
All will know the hand of death,
It may be tomorrow.

For what reason are these things locked in my mind and not other things? May I let them out? If I have indeed longed for death, may I now not do so? What powers do I have to think another way, find another mind for my own, find other words?

No more, I say. I have stayed over-long from what the maid had to say that night. No more of my words, then, but the maid's:

'No, my love, death will not come to us all, but to him it will—death, it may be, in the form of his father, a death he will have sucked in to himself, a death he will play for.

'Some other scholar will tell him of his father, the late king, as seen by a soldier, at night.

'He will go up and out there at night to see for himself, to see his father, and will speak to his father, and his father will speak to him.

'His father will tell him things that have been in his own thoughts, from months before, from the time his father died. (You will remember that time: we will all of us be there at the grave.)'

Indeed it was so. It rained and rained. We stayed whilst the state pastors raised their eyes to pray, one of them touching the shoulder of the dead king's lady (now the king's lady again) with a cold hand, from which she turned away as well as she could.

'We remember before God the soul of this late departed brother, in the hope and expectation that the heavens will receive him, and on the last day, when all will come before their heavenly sovereign....'

But these are words of death again, of which I wish for no more. They are not the maid's, which go on:

'Some time on from then, when the king is there

(the brother of the king as now is: you know, the one that had his arm in a cast), the lady will ask him to wear other clothes, but he will not do so, and never does.

'The king will receive and command, as a king should.

'Two men will come to the youth—to the one that had the late king for a father—and each of them will be another scholar again, like him and the one before. If you could take a look at them —see them as they are, right now—you could well think they wish for nothing but to please him. He'll know better.

'What will truly please him will be the men that come to do a play. He'll know them from before. He'll have one of them redeliver a speech, which your father will not like, but for one of the words.

'He, the young lord as he is by now, will then have them give their play—but with a speech that he's made up for one of them—before the king, the lady and many another: indeed, almost all of you. Not me, as I do not have to say. But you'll be there. This is when you are a young lady. You'll be there, as will he—he'll play with you at the play. With you and with the king. More with the king.

'The king's hand will be held up. The play will

be stayed by the king, for some reason. The king will go out, call for something, and draw you all with him. You'll not know the king's reason for what he does. No-one will. But you'll all think and you'll all fear.

'What was in the play? Was something meant that you had not seen? You'll go over the words of the play in your mind—you and all of them.

'You'll wish you could have seen more of it, but it does not go on to the end. Not this one.

'So the king rises. The play is over. He'll call out some command.

'He, your young lord again, will see the king on his knees. He'll do nothing. When the time comes for him to do something, he will not. He'll do it tomorrow, so he'll tell himself. Take it from me: tomorrow never comes.

'He'll see the lady in a bed chamber, and speak harsh words. His father will come again, and he'll see him, and speak with him, but the lady will not.

'The king will have him go away, with letters that ask for him to be done away with, but he'll see these letters and give them other words, so it'll be the two that are with him that'll end up dead. These are the two that turned up before. I think you know them: they come to play now and again, with you, your brother and the young lord.

'He'll come again to Denmark, and find two other men. They could be, I think, the two from before, them with the letters, but in other clothes. You see, my love, there's more to this than I know of. I do not know what death means here, where the dead may come again—some of them. It may be that I should not say all this to you now, and I would not say it at all if there had been another way, but there is not. You have to know.'

Again words that have stayed in my mind: 'I do not know what death means here.' But it means what it meant for all time, does it not? There is no other death than death. Death is one.

There must be a reason I remember all this. Something here will have to help me.

But I have turned away from the maid's words again, and this time from fear. There are words now that meant more to me than I could quite take in.

'They'll be at a grave.'

She did not say so, but I know this will be *my* grave. There was something of this in my mind at the time, and it comes to my thoughts again and again. How could it not? I will be dead. I will be dead and in my shroud—another of these wretched words I cannot let go of.

If this is not to be, then I have to do something before my time comes. This is the reason for the maid's speech, to tell me that I have to do something if I wish to go on, if I wish to find another path, other words to speak than these words of death.

But they all wish me to be here. I have to be in it with them. As for me, I cannot let them go. How would it be if I left my father, my brother? What would they do? And there's more that I have no wish to be gone from, to have lost to me with no way to restore it. This is where I have my being. This is all I know.

Still, the more I think of these things, the more I know that I would be dead if I stayed here, and which of us could wish for that? There must be some other way, and one day I will find it. All I may do then is hope that all will go well for my father and brother when I have gone. If I stayed I would never know, and if I go I'll never know.

'A master of fashion, with a hat, will come to the young lord from the king, and ask him to take up his sword in commerce of dalliance with your brother.

'In this your brother will come to his death—'

No.

'—and, as he does so, he'll give the young lord reason at last to let his sword find the king. That it will do. The king, as well, will come to his death, and not before time, for by then his lady, she will be dead. Indeed, this is how it is. The lady's death—'

All this death.

'—is what will have made him, the young lord —when he had long denied himself this, and denied his father as well—effect the king's death, the king that will be at the time I now speak of.

'And so then he, your young lord, will come at last to his own death.'

His own death. So here it is. Will it indeed have come in some way from his father, this death? How is it 'his own'? Did *he* make it so? That I could believe. There's death in his words as well. And I could believe he'll have stayed to find his death here, will not have gone away— could not take himself away.

And me, do *I* have my own death that I cannot find a path away from? Is there a death I may find that will be away from here, a death that will be my own, and not one that some other lay down for me? And what other?

'And another king will come. And that will be it.'

She took a breath.
'I wish it did not have to be so, but it does. There's no way out.'
She left.

4

There was one more time when I went with the maid over the mountain, to this hamlet where she had left that daughter she had, and this time my brother was with us. Up we go, up over the mountain, and down where he had not been before. Down, down, down, but now we face the sun.

There's a difference in the green of the grass—but that could be the sun on it. And by the path are some flowers I have not seen before. Flowers have been my love for as long as I remember, and most of them I know. It may be, I think, that the maid would know what they are, but I do not ask. I keep my thoughts in my own mind, my hand in the maid's, and I look over to the left. My brother, I see, is being good, held by the maid's other hand. She had night-things for us all over one shoulder. We are still quite little. Thus we go, each held by the maid, over the mountain.

Let me say what I know of the maid's brother, Mark. He was on his own, and he took in the maid's daughter when she left where she had been before, to come to us. There must have been some reason the maid's daughter did not come to be with us as well, but at the time I did not think of this. I took it as it was. To me, as well, the maid was all.

When she would go to see them, I think it was more to see Mark.

And you could see the joy in *his* eyes. You could see it now as we come down the path and there he is, out of doors, waving to us with his one arm, his left arm—the 'arm that was left', he would say. The other he lost as a soldier. Patient Mark. It could have rained and he would have been there, to see us come.

We go in to see the maid's daughter.

'My daughter'—this from the maid to me, as if we had not seen each other before. And worse, you would think she did not like to have to say these words.

There was, indeed, something a little harsh all the time in how the maid and that daughter would speak to each other. The effect was of two that are not at all close, and have not been so for a long time. For the maid, it may be the daughter was a memory she did not wish to remember. As for the daughter, she stayed by Mark, held him by the hand, as if to keep him there—in his own home! And I did not see this at the time, but it may be she did not like how close I was to the maid.

Well, here we are. We have come. More than before, there's something in the daughter's face I do not like, and we say nothing to one another. Still at night, when we go up to bed, we do not speak. This time we are two in the one chamber, for my brother is in the other. Indeed, we are two in the one bed. We did not speak as we unbraced each other. We did not speak in bed. She did not look at me before she turned over.

Before we had all gone to bed—it was late when we had come there—Mark had given us what it took him all day long to make for us: his 'poor fare', in his words. He was—how was this? —I think he was steward to some lady that had lost most of what she had, but he stayed on, almost out of charity. As a steward he would know how to keep a home: he would know how to wax a table, hard with his arm as the maid did, how to lay things out.

At that table the maid is on my right, then my brother, then Mark (there to hand him things), then the maid's daughter, on my left.

And here's what we had. I give it here as he did at the time, in his own fair hand, as if we had been at the king's table—which indeed we could have been:

Dupped Dove in the fashion of Denmark

Heart of Owl, with rose honey

Beard of Cockle, cold

Heels and Ankle, jangled

Ladies' Joy, larded with rue

Sweet Tongue, on a bed of ground fennel

Puffed Paconcies

Twice-Turned Shoulder of Young Robin, in a stole of rosemary flowers

Valentine's Eyes (which I remember you have to steep in something for a long time, but I cannot remember what)

Saint's Bells, with violets

'Saint's Bells à la maid', Mark would call them, again and again, and at this the maid would look down.

'Fie! Please do not', she would say. 'Not again.'

I remember that night so well: Mark's joy, the glass and other things on the table (all gone now, for the lady is dead and Mark had to go from his home), the maid's 'Not again.' And as I look—as I see now more than I could see then—I see in the maid's eyes a joy like Mark's as she's turned to him, the joy of two as one, the joy of being home. She had a home with us as well. But there's a difference with us. And I think it's from this time on that I come to know what that difference is. This home, here, is more. This is truly a home.

I like most of what we have, but not the beard of cockle. I give mine to the maid. I see my brother does as well.

Then we play Coach and Tenders, and before long we have to go to bed.

'Betime, betime', goes the maid to my little brother. He still could not say it right, and we would say it as he did.

I know we are to go out again in the morning, and I fear the maid's daughter will come with us. But she does not, and, from that look she's given us, I do not believe she would wish to.

My brother rises before me and comes to the chamber where I still have my head down. The maid's daughter lay there by me, quite still. My brother does not come in the bed with us. He would know not to. I help him with his clothes

—that's what he's come for—and we go out of the chamber, heels raised up as we go, whilst I look over my shoulder at the maid's daughter on the bed.

Mark is still in bed: he had had a long hard day. But the maid is up, and we all go out for the morning.

We do not know, my brother and I, where we are to go. We do not mind: the maid must know, for she treads on, face to the heavens and the morning, with one of us again in each hand.

It's cold. My eyes weep.

So we come, on the path that would redeliver us home tomorrow, to a green door in the mountain—a grass-green door we did not see the day before. Was it there?

Without knocking we go in: the door falls away at the maid's raised hand, to close again when we have all come in to this chamber.

There is no window, and all I may make out in there is the pale breath of some other being.

'This is the Lady Profound.' The words are the maid's.

'She's not a Christian, is she?' I ask. I cannot think what made me do so—as if I did not know what the Lady Profound was. Some fear it must have been.

'No, my love. She may see what cannot be seen. She may tell what no other hath powers t' tell.'

From my brother there comes nothing. We all go down, knees on the ground. We know right away, my brother and I, that this is what we have to do.

I see now in the maid's hand some violets. I see the maid give these to the Lady Profound—and indeed this is she, the one that all speak of but not so many have seen. And now, as my eyes tune in to the little that comes from some wax in a glass at the lady's right ankle, I see the Lady Profound.

What may I say? All I remember is an effect of pale green, a piteous look, an owl on one shoulder. But more than this I cannot say.

Then it comes to seem that she will speak, and she does so by means of the owl: what she would wish to say comes as the owl's speech.

It's hard to look at this owl, it's so wretched and cold, held there in a false night, day in and day out. But it's hard not to look, when what you may see is an owl with the command of speech:

'Expectancy i'-i'-is a mould o'-o'-on the ha'-ha'-hand, and remembrance nothing. Take up the snow o'-o'-of now. Take i'-i'-it in your ha'-ha'-hand and see it go. This i'-i'-is the death of now, and this is all now i'-i'-is: now is not so long that you may say 'now'. It's o'-o'-over. Come up and see me some time.'

I see the owl's eyes now. They do not seem to know what goes on here. These words do not come from them. They look out at us as if there's no mind in there.

We say nothing, my brother and I. We each look to the maid to tell us what to do. She does not seem to be at all affrighted by the Lady Profound and the owl, but we find it hard to be quite so composed. We did what it seemed we had to do. We stayed still, knees on the ground, as if to pray. The maid answers—not to the owl but to the Lady Profound:

'We are here to know more than thy blasted moan. We have come all this way for thy counsel.'

I think the Lady Profound—the Lady Profound's owl, that is—will speak again. Then I think she—it—will not. Then I do not know. Then the words come:

'A'–a'-ask what you will a'-a'-ask. T'-t'-take what you will t'-t'-take. Know what you will know. Play it again, Sun.'

The maid rises to this, rises from the ground, and so do we:

'No more of these daisy thoughts! We have to have thy help—as thou and thy speech-master well know. These two young things I have with me, they have to have thy help—one of them most of all. Speak what thou must to them, not what thou'll like to.'

'S'-s'-speech i'-i'-is locked and cannot be blown here and there, one way and another, by the will. Not by your will and not by mine. T'-t'-take mind: you have no way to find for yourself what to say; you cannot do so. There is one that lay down your words for you. And mine. Do not blame my words, for I did not make them up. They are made for me, as i'-i'-indeed are yours for you. Truly, my sweet, I do not give a doublet.'

The maid by now is up and waving a hand as if to wish the Lady Profound would go away.

'I do not believe this.'

'Believe what you will. Think what you will. Do what you will. I'-i'-it will all come out as i'-i'-it must. Do not be deceived by hope, for hope i'-i'-is fouled stockings. You have not seen nothing ye—'

Then the maid—and I still cannot quite believe

it, never mind that I was there—with a raised arm goes at the Lady Profound, and in the knocking and the shaking and the waving of the two of them, the wax falls and goes out. Now we may see nothing.

This goes on for some time. I look at my brother. I believe he took a look at me. But we cannot see each other, no more than we may see the maid and the Lady Profound and the owl, all tumbled, as we think, on the ground, where the maid and the Lady Profound have a go at each other. What will come of all this?

I do not know if the maid had been here before. I would think she was here one time. So she would know what to do. But she did not say. And is this the way to go on with the sovereign lady of the night?

My brother and I say nothing. I bended over to him and held his hand. Hard to believe that out there it was still morning, whilst here, in the night, these two tear at one another. Now they seem to be down on the ground; now they are up again. This goes on and on.

At length they come to an end and are composed again, almost so, the maid with us and the Lady Profound where she was. Their breath is harsh-blown. I see the Lady Profound make the wax go again. We do not know quite how—no-one will say—but the one that lost was the Lady Profound. This means—we had to make this out, my brother and I, at home again—that now the Lady Profound will have to speak some more, and this time speak true.

She does so. Well, the owl does so.

'The daughter of the cold green mountain does not know which path of two she should take. Should she go to the right and do what she will? Should she go to the left and do what she must? More: is there a difference? What answers will she give? There is more than one lesson she will have to find out, you see. She cannot say which way to go whilst she may see but one, the one she is on now. She will have to come to the other. But which is that? The will, the must? Will she find out? Must she find out? What help may she hope for? Little from me. Little from you. Little, so little, from that brother she is with. There is another, another that will show the other way. Let the daughter of the cold green mountain look for him—if indeed it is a him, which it may not be. More I cannot say. More you must not ask for. More you will not ask for.'

I may not remember this speech quite as it was, but I know these words are close to it, for most of them are locked away in my memory, to take out now and again for a perusal. They are words that —as was my hope—have meant more than I could see in them at the time. As the months go by, it will come to me that there are two key things for me to keep in mind from that morning: the words, and how it was that the maid took me to see the Lady Profound. She must have had a reason. She had given me something in that night-time speech of death and the end; now she had given me something more.

As for the words, I would think more and more of the one that was to show me the way, the one that was to help me. Could it be my father, as at one time it seemed to me it must be? If so, when would his help come? And what was the reason it could not come now? If not my father, was it Gis? The king? The maid's brother? There are not so many more men I know. But then, as the Lady Profound's words left it, the one that helps could be a she.

Now I know the one it is. Now I know it must and it will be one I did not know at that time, one that would be with me some day, one I did not have to look for, one that would come, one that is now here.

With that, it seemed that this counsel from the Lady Profound was over. She let a little time go by. Then the owl, to show this was the end, did speak one last time:

'What you have had from me is—', and then it goes by letters, as if this is one of the words it cannot say, 'T-A-B-O-O. Do not speak of this to another soul.'

The maid's eyes are still on the Lady Profound as she rises up: 'We will not.'

'All of you.'

So we all—and we all are up now—say these words again: 'We will not.'

'You have promised, as a soldier on his sword.'

'We have promised, as a soldier on his sword.'

'Go!'

That was it. No 'fare you well'. Nothing of that. No more gifts as we left.

Being out of the green door again, out in the sun now—it blasted my eyes—we left to take the path to Mark's home again, the maid and then us two. We did not think it right to speak. Nothing more did we two say that morning. When you are little there are things you know to do, and not make an argument of it, not ask for a reason. But this time there was a reason: the maid had to think. There she was, before us, head down, eyes down. And us two, on the path, quite still, hand in hand.

Never again did we speak of this access we had had to the Lady Profound. But late that night, when we had gone up to bed and the maid held out my night-shirt for me, there was a look she had. If I close my eyes, I may see it still, that look, that hard look, as if to say: 'Remember'.

I do. And before that night is over I will see in my mind's eye so many things I do not know—one upon another, now this, now that—that it is as if there are bells all over the chamber, as if my head will be blasted by the music of them.

There are bells that sing a jangled ground and the end of another day, bells of blame and beauty, dalliance and doubt, bells of glass, blown bells, cast bells, bells shaking and knocking, bells Christian and other, bells of pastors, of Sundays, of death and remembrance, bells that keen, bells that keen for a god gone, bells of things and thoughts tumbled out of tune, bells of horrors, of a wish that was denied, of charity fouled, bells from the dead of night, bells of before and again, bells that do no more than tell the time, bells at doors, bells of givers when they could not be patient, bells of a cold morning on the mountain, bells that speak like one sword on another, bells of flowers, of columbines waving in the morning, bells of a tongue touching memory, bells to restore to us months in a day, bells on the arm of a fair lady as she rises to sing, at the ankle of a young king in a state of fear, on the sandal of a saint as she goes up to pray, bells that tell the steward when he must obey, bells that tell a daughter what she had to know.

5

To see a fair lady upon a night coach.
Stone on the right hand and bells on the heels,
She shall have music when

When indeed there still *was* music. When my brother was still a little primrose. Then I would sing to him like this, and we could go on all morning that way, when we had done with the other things we had to say to each other.

And when I speak of my brother at this time —of how he was and of how I was with him— I have to say I did good things for him, never mind what was to come. I did all that was in my powers for my brother. Remember: I was young as well. I may see now that there was more I could have done, more I could have given him—but not then. Then I left nothing out; then there was nothing that could have been done that I did not do. I did not have to think what to do: I let love show me how. And if I had it to do all over again, there would be no difference.

Still, I must take some of the blame for how things turned out with him for a time.

Young King Poll
Was a merry young soul,
And a merry young soul are you.
He did call for his grass,
And did call for his owl,
And did call for his ladies two.

With my father away for months on end, and the other one—*she*—being as she is, it falls to me and the maid to do what we may for my brother—to give him the love and affection a young one should have.

It was right we did that. I cannot think it was not. And it was *his* right. We had to do what we could to make up for what was not there.

But I know now that we could never, alack, give him all the things he should have had from my father, not to speak of the other one. Do what we may, we cannot. And this becomes more true as the months go by. We see it.

'It was nothing you did', I say. 'Father's not himself this morning.'

'If he's not himself, then what *is* he?'

'Not himself. That's all. It's something you say.'

'I know. I remember. You tell me again and again. It's something you say.'

'Would you like to come with me up the mountain?'

'No.' He will not look at me.

'Do you have a reason?'

'No.'

'Is it what I had to say to you last night?'

'No.'

'Will you come tomorrow?'

'No.' Still his eyes are down on the ground.

'Will you come another day?'

'No.'

> *Tumbled, tumbled, little sun,*
> *How I think what you have done,*
> *Up a*

But I cannot see—cannot see where it will come from, and when: this cold breath of fear. In the months when it rained, there we would be: him by himself (I would know not to go up there), and me on my own as well. I look out of the window, at how it rains, and I think. Then he'll come in and ask me, sweet as could be, to go with him to the music chamber, which they keep locked, but I have the key. I know what he's come for: all he would have to do would be come in and look at me. In the music chamber is a little table, where she let us play Go. For Go whiles away the time; Go would give us something to do other than think.

You cannot play Coach and Tenders with two, but Go you may. Indeed, for Go you have to have two and no more. That's one of the things I remember from a time I do not like to remember. You have to have two. So he had to have me.

I think my father must have seen more than he seemed to at the time. One morning he turned to us to say he would find a Go master for us, 'being as how you play Go all day long'. That was so like him: if we did something, we had to do it well. And that was how I took it at the time.

He did not let time go by. Before we know where we are, we are at the table in the music chamber, and here's this Go master to give us a lesson.

'Right. Go One-O-One.

'You must have another with you to play Go, as

you know. This is not something your honourable brother may do by himself; this is not something you, honourable lady, may do without him. For each of you, there must be the other. In Go, you are locked to each other. It must be so. Locked to each other and locked away. It must be as if you two are all there is in all of time.

'You may play green, honourable lady. If not, then you, honourable youth, must play green. One of you must play green, the other the other. There is no other way.'

His right hand, there, on the table.

'You may speak as you play, but you do not have to. For Go you do not have to have words at all.' Indeed, that was good for us.

'But to go on— Ha! *Go* on!' My brother let out a sigh 'Well, to go on, you take up one of your men in your hand, like this.' And he was touching my hand. I draw it away, no more than a little, and he lets go. Ha. No more of that.

'And indeed your men may be lost that way. This is the way of Go. They come, they go.' Another sigh from my brother.

'Where was I? So, indeed. You must not let the other take them! Keep that in mind! See how here your honourable brother could take you? And he will! And if he does, you will have lost face. So you have to think.

'There is a way to make your play well, and more than one way to do it other than well. It may take you months to find a good way to play one of your men—and still there will be a better. You may never find that way. You may wax and pale and never find it. That would be wretched for you—and it will be more wretched if you come close to the way and still cannot find it, but know it is there and you cannot find it, know that you could go on and on and never find the way.

'If you are to have a better hope that you will, one day, find the way, then Go must have all of your mind. All of your mind must be Go-mind. That's all there is to it. That's all I have to say on that one. So please: play Go and do not think of these other things. It's better that way. This is the way to—'

'Go!'

That was my brother. Like the owl of the Lady Profound's.

Cock a daisy do,
My lady's lost two shoon,
My master's lost his fennel staff
And does not know what to do.

I have my hand on his little shoulder.

'Do not do that.'

I keep my hand there.

'Do not do that, *please*.'

Still I keep my hand there.

He turned, and as he did so, my hand falls.

Rains, rains, go away:
Come again another day.

Another day, when we have gone out, he treads before me up the mountain, and does not look to see where I may be. All the way he never turned. By the time we come to the mountain's brow— where in months gone by we would play all the long morning—we are quite puffed out. We look out yonder—that way to the watchman's ha-ha, and over there to where the holy men have their home, and so on down to Twice-Way Green. There is no sun: late that day it rained, I remember. We go down again, again with him before me.

That may have been the morning when father, as was his way, held up his hand to say we would all go away to find some sun—I cannot remember where. I wish we had done that more, for things are better with my brother and me when we are away. For what reason I do not know: I take it as it comes.

It may be there's more to be observed when one's away, so that the two of us are little observers of this and that all day long: how they make flowers in bended glass (and you have to see them as they do it); the way men will look at things before they take them, touching them all over; the holy well that you may look down and see no end; all the things they have in the baker's window; the Hope Falls (a must-see). We would go from one of these things to another, him and me, and he would tell me his thoughts—of what we had seen, and other things. It seemed he could speak truly to me again, tell me of himself as he did before. But at home it was never like that now.

There's never an argument. It's not that. It's more that we keep touching on things that we each know the other does not wish to speak of.

The Go time is long over, and if we are in the music chamber now it's indeed to play music. With music, thank God, you cannot speak. But when two of you play music, you may say things to each other you could never say in words, and that may not be so good.

Did I say before—I think I did—that my brother was better than me at music? That was all right; I would like it when I would come home to find he had gone there to play by himself, for by now he had a key of his own, and I could go in, and him not see me. But when it's the two of us, he *does* mind that I play worse, and he does *not* keep his thoughts to himself. There would be a raised shoulder, a look—most of the time with no words, so we could have given the effect, to one that did not know us and did no more than look in from the door, that all was well. It was not.

There was something by Beard we would play then: 'Boré in B'. It was hard for me, and if we had a go at it late at night—as we would, when my father, the maid and *she* had all gone to bed—I would find I was out of breath some way before the end.

'Come on!' This was him. 'And give it more affection! This *grave* means it should be noble: you take it more like death!'

I would say nothing to this. I took it as his way, no more than that. I could wish he had been more patient, and it made me fear for him: it's not good to see how your own brother becomes unkind, ungracious. But there it is: he was no saint.

Then, if we should play it over again. I would be worse than before. For him, that would be it. At something out of tune from me, it would all be over. He would be up, and then, with an oath, he would go.

It was no better when I could keep up with him, and not come in late. We would go on to the end, but all his jangled thoughts would come out in the music.

What did in Cock Robin?
'I', the owl did say,
'When you had gone away,
I did in Cock Robin.

From when was it like this? There had been a time, long before, when we did not speak at all, and when the music chamber stayed locked— when all the commerce we had was by means of brief letters. These we meant for my poor father: we would take them up to him. I have some of them with me still:

(Not all of them are well composed; we are so young at the time.)

'My brother recks it all.'

'If O goes to heaven, I would like to go to hell.'

'He will never obey me, and he must not play with my perfume. I will not have it.'

'My grace'—I think he meant 'glass'—'is my own. Tell O.'

'Keep you-know-what out of my chamber. And make him give me the sandal he stole.'

'I done not take O's violets. No how.'

'What is the purport of these letters if my brother cannot rede?'

'I do not like to go with O to the mountain.'

Rosemary pale, daisy, daisy,
Rosemary green,
When you are king, daisy, daisy,
I shall be keen.

But keen as I still would be all this time to help my brother, it comes to seem to me more and more that there's little hope. We had been almost one being. Now we are two—and two that do not know one another, never mind two that had some affection for each other, for I could not show my love now and he seemed to have lost his.

Worse was the doubt. Had we truly had what I think we did? How could that sweet little brother of my memory have turned in to this? I come to fear I know nothing of my brother and never did. And that will make me fear there's nothing of which I may say: 'This is true'. If not him, then what may I keep and know that I have? What may I close my hand over and never let it go?

Had I let *him* go when I did not have to, when I could have done something but did not? Had I let him down? If so, it would have been at the time *she* left. And now I would have to make up for it in some way: that was all I could think. As to how, nothing I did was quite right. I could see that. I could tell there was a way I could not find, words I could not say—words that would have made a difference to him. So it went on. If I could find the words now, late as it is, I believe it would still help—help him and help me. If I could say—no more than this—something of what was in my mind at the time, that could do some good. But, again and again, when I say something to him, it comes out cold and false.

It may be I should let time do what must be done: there's reason to hope it will.

As for the time of which I speak, all he will say is that now he's being himself, and, if I do not like it, I do not like him. No more than that.

'You never remember, do you? You never know what it means. I do not love you. I do not like you.'

This little bore's gone to mark it,
This little bore stayed at home.
This little bore took dupped dove,
This little bore had non,
And this little bore did weep 'O, o, o!'
All the way home.

6

When my father was away, be it for no more than a day and a night, I would receive letters from him, and these I would look at over and over again, my hand touching the words, lay them where my brother could see (and he would let me see his), and then keep in my closet where no-one could find them.

That was where, at one time, I would keep all the things that meant most to me: some violets given me by a young soldier, now withered but still with a little perfume to them; a Valentine from another (we had been at the watchmen's hey and had gone out to see the night); a stone; a sovereign; a glass heart from I do not remember where; a little wheel my brother had made.

The letters are there still, with all the other things, so I will take them out and look at them from time to time. But most of them I remember by heart.

'My daughter,

'All is well. My tongue is better, and so are my eyes. It all turned out to be nothing. No doubt it did me good that I stayed in bed for a day before I had to go away.

'The fashion here you would not believe! And what they give you each night! Night on night all I have had was heart!

'I have given my speech now: I did so from memory. If you like, I will give it when home with you, so you may see how well I do it. What I had to say of Honour and the State Good did, I must say, go truly well. It made the king himself say he would like to know more! I'll see him before I go.

'With all a father's love.'

He was a master of the speech. Never—of this there may be no doubt—did he give other than a good one, and he could do so when he had to speak on something that was not at the time close to his heart.

Many of them I remember, as well as I remember his letters: the speech on Love and Affection he did for the maid and the baker, the one on What To Give To Charity for the Chamber of

Commerce, the one on *Dead Souls* that's gone down so well each time with the pastors of All Saint's. But if I should redeliver them, I could not do it the way *he* did it.

If he had to give a state speech here, we would all be there. It would be a day of joy for us: me, my brother (most of the time), the maid, for as long as she was with us. Not the other one: she would never come.

He could make a speech that was quite brief, but most of the time he did not. He held you. And you would wish he would go on to morning.

When a speech by him was promised, never mind where, they would come from all over to be there, all of them with expectation in their eyes. You would see a green youth by one with a beard, a soldier by a music head, two keen observers by some beauty in a stole. They would all be quite still for as long as he would speak. Each face would show the effect he made: woe at this, joy at that. Then he would draw it all to a close, and you could almost see the words take form as he did so, and how could all there not then give him a good hand?

If I close my eyes, I see my father at one such time. He rises. All is still. His right arm is raised, and there is a look in his eyes as if his thoughts could still be in doubt. Then his hand falls and he's away.

It was something to remember, being at a speech of his. The letters he would receive! 'I was there the night you made your speech on such and such.' 'Thank you for your words, thank you.' 'Here was something for me to tell my daughter one day.' 'You have such powers with words you could prove two and two make one.'

We would be there at the door to take him home when his speech was done, and they would be all over him. He had something to say to each, and would never sigh as they would go on and on with their good thoughts of him and his speech, but would look at them, with his patient eyes.

Daughter mine,
My tongue is, ay me, not so good. You would think I had been given something rich, but all it was —as, indeed, on each day I have been here— was more heart!

My shoulder, as well, is not so good as it was before.

But my eyes now are indeed better. I may see what effect I make when I give a speech. And think of this: I have to speak to His Majesty himself on Reason and Command! I'll be in ecstasy!

'I'll say more of this.
'My love to you all.'

Poor father, he was never quite well. These things with his heart and his shoulder I remember, for he would tell us of them each morning, but do so in a merry way. He's still like that. He'll come down, say what's not right with him and make little of it, and I'll say: 'Poor father!' And he'll say: 'No, no: rich, rich!' It's one of the things I love him for.

If he stayed in bed all day—as he would tell me he did in some of these letters, and as he did at home—then in no way was that for himself: I wish it had been. No, it was to fashion his words, to think how he could redeliver some speech from before and make it better still. These are things he would have to do by himself, away from us, and where better than in bed? That was where he composed, then as now. 'That's where words come to me', he would say. 'I find them in the bed clothes.'

I wish he had been well more of the time. The end of his tongue had a little green mould on it for months, but he took it with a good grace. Another time, when he had something not right with his eyes, he could not make out letters from a table's length away. How I would wish I could take some of this on my shoulders!

'Please,' I would say, 'have this day to yourself. Give no mind to us. Go out up the mountain: that would do you good.'

And he would say, his words touching my heart: 'No, no, nothing turned in the still mind. You know how it is with me: when there's a speech to be done, I cannot keep away from it.' And then there would be all the other things he had to do.

He was hard on himself, and that cannot have been a help to his eyes, which have never been good. His left arm, as well, had little play in it.

This was all from the time when he, like so many men, was a soldier. The maid's brother Mark was in my father's command, and—this I had from Mark, not from my father, for he would say little of his youth—the two of them had been blasted by a mine as they had gone to take something up to the king's watchman. I remember Mark's words:

'It was night time, and quite still. Then all hell rained down on us from the mountain. Your father and I are out cold. We did not come to for a long time: another two had to come out to find us. Then, as we lay there, your father turned to me. He could not speak, but he did give me a look, as if to say: "Are you all right?" '

'My daughter,
'It's late now, but I had to tell you a little of my thoughts before I turned in.

'My speech before the king on Reason and Command did, I must say, go better than when I did it before. His Majesty stayed for most of it. And Lord Last—he was there as well, for as long as the king was—Lord Last had this to say: "I think your thoughts most noble, most noble", before he had to go. You must know how this would please me!

'Now I have more to do for them—a speech which I think I will call: "Should the Poor Blame the Rich?" It may be hard to make this go as it should.

'What I took for my eyes does indeed help— which is good when each day I have to make another speech!

'As for my tongue, it's better now, but my heart is not so good. There may be reason for this: the fare we had late at night this time was not heart but...tongue!

'Let me know if you receive this. I'll give it to one of Lord Last's little men, me being so well in with him now.

'Tenders to you all.'

I do not know what I would do without him.

Daughter mine,
I think of you and love you. I think, as well, of Little.
Is he being good?
    It may be that I will not see you all for some time,
and if so, there is something I would like you to tell
him from me, if and when he must go away from
home. This is what I would say:
    ' "Give your thoughts no tongue.
    ' "What men you know, and that show you affec-
tion, you should keep by you.
    ' "Give each lord your shoulder, but no madam
your heart.
    ' "Do not take and do not give. You know what this
means.
    ' "Look good when you go out, but doubt fashion.
    ' "This most of all: to your own soul be true, and it
must come from this, as night from day, you may not
then be false to rich, to poor."
    As to that, I think the speech I must give here may
now be: "Do the Poor Shame the Rich?" I'll see.
    But please give these words to Little as they are.
Speak them as I would speak them. You know how.
They are noble words and should be done in a noble
way. Do them from memory, if you may. Have them
by heart. And keep them in your own heart.

'As for my heart, it is better, and so are my tongue, shoulder and eyes. I pray God that you are well, that all of you are well.

'There are thoughts that I have, now and then, that are hard to say to you. I would like to say more, but may not.

'With a father's love and affection.'

It was so like my father that he should give his mind most to another, as here to my brother, when he was away from home—when he had a speech to think of, when he had to look out all the time for what was being made of him by men in command, and when he had, as well, these day-to-day things with his heart, his eyes and so on.

I never had to redeliver that counsel to my brother. As it turned out, there was nothing to keep my father from us for long. But it was good to have the words down where I could see them, and think of them, and think of how he would speak them, and so think of him when he was away. They are words to call him to mind— words he's never but been true to. He never lets himself down. And if that means he never lets himself go, it's not up to me to wish he would. But I do. There's no chamber in his heart where he is king.

'My daughter,

'Lord Last was here to see me. Think of that! And more: Lord Little was with him! Such good men. They would have stayed and stayed, I do believe, but had to be away. I think now my speech will be: "How the Poor are to Blame".

'I was up late at a show. I know you do not like the music I like; still, I think you would like this from what they did:

Love, love me do,
You know I love you,
I'll never be true,
So PLEASE, love me do.

'Well, you have to know the music. It's not at all like the king's: I'll play it for you when home—which is where I long to be!

'My tongue, heart and eyes are all well. Not so my shoulder, but never mind.

'With more of your father's love, and more to come.'

This was long before the late king died. My father was good at music, when he had the time. He would play and sing with us, and have us go over things for him before a lesson. If he could, he stayed for the lesson, and that made a difference to the lady that had come to coach us. With him there, she would find a way to make you play better. 'I think you lost the argument a little there, where it goes to another key.' 'May this be more like bells?' 'Think of this, that you have gone out in the morning to make music, and here, in the right hand, you sing as the sun rises over the mountain.' As for him, he did not have to speak.

'Daughter mine,
'His Majesty could not be there when I made my speech. But all was well.

'Lord Last and Lord Little did not come. They had given me help with it—which could well have given them their reason not to come! There was nothing in it that they did not know!

'There was a Madam Something that was there, and stayed for all my speech. And His Grace did indeed come—did I tell you of His Grace? And Lord Say and another noble lord with their daugh-ter. I did not know that a lord by himself, with another lord, could have a daughter, but there we are.

'So that was all.

'But I do not mind. Better a good speech to a poor soul than a poor speech to a good—

'No, that's not it.

'I should be in bed by now. It's late, and I'll be home with you before long. I'll tell you more then.

'May the grace of God be with you, and a father's heart's love.'

7

I think it was a little before these letters that *she*
—the lady of this little home that was no home
for as long as she stayed there—went.

Most of the day, by now, she lay in bed, in a
chamber away from my father's. The reason was
not—as with my father—so that she could do
letters and things like that. No. No.

There was a time before. I know there was. I
have to keep that in mind. There was a time when
I could go in and out of their chamber, when the
two of them had the one chamber, which was
where my brother and I had come in to being. I
could go in and out without fear, never think.

That's now my father's: he had stayed there
when she took all she had to another chamber.

She had, in effect, left him—but not gone.

Up there she would call in men—men such as

he would never receive. She was quite reckless. She had no wish at all to keep it from my father. And he could not make the lady keep it from my brother and me.

It may be that one day I'll find it piteous. But not now.

So that's how it was. I was in on it, and so was my brother. How could he not be? It was as if she had this wish to be observed. No, not observed. She had to have us know what went on, know what she was—know and have no-one to tell, so that we would have to make it seem there was nothing at all. It was a way to shame shame.

I remember young Robin, flaxen-head Robin, Robin that was so young he had no beard, bare-faced Robin. He would have seemed a sweet youth to me had it not been for what he did— and how he was. He would come knocking on the door each day at two, and I would be the one that had to let him in.

'Hey,' he would say, 'how's things?'

No time for answers. Right away he would have turned from me to go up, touching my shoulder with his hand as he went. That hand.

Then down he would come. I did not like the

look on his face, the way he held himself. Quite the young courtier.

This was before the time when two of the night watchman's staff would come in the morning, and *she* would be with them most of the day. I did not know what to call them. What *she* would call them was Other and Another.

They had a key she had given them, so I did not have to see them all the time as I did Robin, which was all right by me. But I did know they had gone up to their lady love: there was the sigh, the moan, from the door—from the bed. Then I would go up the mountain and not come down again before they had gone. And I would take my brother with me, for as long as I could make him go.

But, do what we would, we could not help but see these two now and again, here and there, for they had their home close by. And they are there still. They look at me as if nothing had gone on.

They are men—not like Robin. She had gone on to men. They have, as she would say, the bulk of men.

By now she would tell me what she did with them. I had the call to go up there one day, before they had come. Did I know what went on? I did.

Never mind, she had to tell me face to face what she was up to. And she had to tell me again from time to time, and still with that look she had.

'I do not know which I like more'—this was one time—'of Other and Another. You know them. Which do you like the look of?'

What did she think I could say to this?

She went on.

'Other is fair—heavenly fair from his head to his heels, all over, my Being Beauteous.'

She seemed to like to speak words like this, and know that as she did so she fouled them.

'I like it as well when he's turned away from me, when I know his fair eyes and all the other fair, fair things of him are there, but cannot see them. I know I'll see them again, all right. I know I'll see each feature of him, that he'll give himself to my perusal: he'll have to. And all the time he'll say nothing, for they know what I like, these two.

'They never speak to me, and they never speak to each other. That's the way I like it, and that's the way it will have to be.'

And I had to see all this, how she would be. I could not close my eyes.

'*I* must be the one to speak. *I* must be the one to give them the lesson they have come for—each day another lesson, each day some difference.

They like it that there's this difference in what we do, and it does something for me as well, to keep them on their form.'

I still cannot quite believe she could say all this to me.

' "Lesson" did I say? I'll come to that. So, they do not speak. Each of them I know to have a tongue in his head, and a sweet, sweet tongue at that. No, they have lost nothing. They have the means to speak. They have, indeed, all the means.

'As for Another, on his face there's more of a down-cast look. He is night to Other's day; and where with Other you see the sun come out, with Another it's as if it rained, and all you would wish to do now is go in, go in with him, and have your way with him whilst the rains go on.

'Take a look at him some time. How could you not wish and hope the rains would never end?

'With him the night comes over you: he will take you in to his night, and with his hand he will make the sun go out. There is the still of night in him. And there are the powers of night.

'His stature is that of a god, the god of night. Indeed he is a god, made to command. But he does not. I do.'

I remember the look she had; I see these eyes as they held me. How could she do this, given what she must see in my face: a daughter's love?

Daughter? Before long she lost all that from me.

'He will give himself to me, and he will give me his powers of night, the powers in his arm. That arm: I have seen it shaking as he held me—shaking in ecstasy. Believe it.

'So here they are, Other and Another, my men. As I say, I do not know which I like more. And I do not have to know, for I may have the two of them—one by one if I wish, but most of the time as they will be when you have gone: the two of them with me in my chamber, on my bed, as night and day, the sun and the rains. My two men, made for me.

'And, as well, I do not know—do not have to know—which I like more out of being observed and being one of the observers. Other and Another and me: that will make two thrice over. Other and me. Another and me. And—o heaven! —Other and Another.

'Each of us may be observed and observers at the one time in what we do. This way, that way. Your way, his way. Their way, my way.

'But when it's their way—when I look at one and see in his eyes what he'll most like to do to me, have done to him—it's still my way. If I do things to please them, as I do most of the time —not all—, it's to please me as well.

'We may all be givers. We may all be given. They may give to each other, and they may give to me as they do so. I will give what I will. I will take what I will. I will keep them so that they long for what I will give and what I will take.

' "Out of your clothes!" I may say, to the two of them. If not, I may have one of them keep his clothes on—some of his clothes—for it may be better that way. I could make each of them take the other out of his clothes, and give them some music to do so. You should see it!

'It's good, as well, when you do this yourself, take them out of their clothes. They like that. And they should like what you do to them. But you should like it more.

'They'll do as I ask: there's never a doubt of that. They do all I ask.

' "Look at me!" "Do not look at me!" "Let's see that again!"

'Let's say it's like this: each of them will take himself out of his shirt, his long stockings (for I like them to wear stockings most of the time), and so on. I may sigh, I may moan, to please them. They know I do it for them, and do not mind. How should they mind? They are mine.

'Then the lesson will go on. "Find another way so that he's held where he is!" "In there!" "Not so close: I'll tell you when!" "How steep may you make it go?" "Do you remember when you did that with it before?" "Not his, mine!" "Give it to me here, now!" I will come again another time for more.

'But do I have to go on? The words you know as well as I do, but not, I think, what each of them means. Have no fear, that will—shall I say?—come.

'So: Come.' So the words indeed come, and at each she took another look at me. 'Beauty. Tumbled. Breath. Tumbled beauty, tumbled breath. Hand. Touching. Cock. Hard. Each of them with a hard-on. Long long long. Draw. Draw in. Ecstasy. To be dupped and dupped again. To be dupped by the one and then by the other, and then by the one again, for as long as it will take that you cannot remember which is which. To have them look and look and find the doors, find all the doors. Call out. More. More. Now. To be gyved. To be jangled. To be larded. To be larded all over and in me. To be done. To be well and truly done.'

Was she done with this now? Did she think I had had all I could take? No, there would be more another day, and more again.

Did she know what she had done? She had made it so that I could not believe my own memory. I could not now believe I truly could remember: I was left in a cold night of doubt.

Some things I had that I held on to. My father, most of all—now that my brother had gone his own way and the maid had left us. My father would show me what is right and true, and what it means to be right and true in yourself.

But him, as well, she would have fouled in my mind if she could. She would tell me things that may have been true, but things I had no wish to know, and indeed no *right* to know. It was a way to show the powers she had over me.

'Your father is nothing. I know he may have had some thoughts of being made a lord, but the king, you know, does not love him, not truly. It's all for show, for the good of the state. To the king he's no more than another courtier. The king will let him go when he's done with him. That's how it is. That's how these things go.'

This is the king that was.

'There was a day, indeed, when the king held your father in some honour. But that day is long gone. It may still please them—the king and his ungracious lady—to keep your father by them, but you should see how they make a face at each other when he cannot see. Do not be deceived. We all know it: he's a bore. But they like to play with him. They love it when they make him show himself up. And then there's this, that they think he may know more than he should.

'That would be from before. Now he's nothing. His powers are over.'

The way she puffed out that 'powers': it was as if she longed to have him blown to nothing.

It was not all false. It was false in how it was meant. She would have had to know she could never have an effect on my love for my father, and could never make him seem little in my eyes. Still, she made a difference. I would look at him, my own father, with all the love I had for him, and could not say what was on my mind. And we had been so close before. We would be so again when she was gone and out of the way, but still then—still now—there are things I cannot tell him. And I see in his eyes how they seem to ask me for a reason, as they show me his love.

I could not and cannot tell him. So she is still here, one cold hand on each of us, when we speak. I could not and cannot tell him how some of the things she did would make me fear I had lost my reason—how she would then come to me at night, and speak as if she could never have been unkind to me.

'My daughter, my daughter, let me lay my hand on your brow whilst you tell me all your thoughts.'

How could I then draw away? How could I not show affection, now that she seemed to show some for me? And if by this time I could not find affection in my heart, how could I not *seem* to show it? So there I was, sucked in to a play, made to show a false face.

It was not for nothing that I almost lost my mind. If *she* was like this, was that so of them all? My father? My brother? The maid? The young soldier with violets in his hand? Did they all do what they did for show, for me to see? No more than that?

I had to make my way from door to door, touching each with a brief hand.

I remember Sundays. I remember these wretched Sundays, when there was no lesson to take my mind away to other thoughts, and the maid had by now gone away with the baker, and my father would have to keep at it with some speech, and my brother would play music as long as I let him be (he had 'O Keep Out!' on the music chamber door, to which I had lost my key), and it was she and me.

One such day comes to mind more than most. It was late in the morning, and she and I had done what we had to: take the things from the table, see to father's clothes (this was something she would still do for him, and I would like to help). All the time she did not speak to me. Now we had nothing to do but look at one another, and as she held me with these two cold eyes, she sucked on a stone. That was all. Still she did not speak—did not *have* to speak. She sucked on a stone.

In the still of the late morning there was an expectation—and that look, that cold look, had my heart knocking. I have to do something. She will not. It's up to me. She will go on and on there, with that look held on me, and do nothing. There's nothing she'll have to do. I have lost my ground right away, my heart knocking, my hand shaking. All she will have to do is be patient.

So I tumbled out my woe. What reason could I

have had to do so? This: that there was not one soul I could have turned to. My brother now was on his own path, and as it turned out, I would never again find a way to tell him my close thoughts: things went another way. My father—well, she had made it hard for me to speak to him. And the more she held me with that look, the more it seemed I had to say what was on my mind. So I tumbled out my woe to the one that had given me that woe. I had lost all hope.

I never did this again, but I wish I had not given in then. I should have had the powers of mind to face the lady out, play it quite cold. But I could not. If I had it to do over again, then I could find such powers, for there's more to me now than the poor, sweet daughter. But with that look on me, and no-one to give me a hand, I could not.

A pale stone. She took it out and held it, and turned it in the sun, so that she could look at it as I went on and on. She did so to show me how little my words meant, now that she had made me speak. But that made me go on the more. And so my shame becomes the more.

I see me there. I see me weep. I see me go on with my words, my jangled words, more and more out of breath.

O, if you could have held your tongue!

She rises whilst I still speak on, on and on. She goes out.

She was a length of hell.

I know the time will come when the glass of my memory will close over, when I will see nothing in it, know nothing, and then I must not fear but be quite still and patient, whilst my remembrances come to me again, one by one. And as my memory becomes composed again, so will I.

Mine is a memory made, as all memory is made, of what was and what should have been. Wish is close to memory, and will find a way in. Wish will not be denied. We all know that. Your memory is not one but many—a long music you have made and will make again, over and over, with some things you know and some you do not, some that are true and some you have made up, some that have stayed from long before and some that have come this morning, some that will go tomorrow and some that have long been there but you will never find them, not if you look from now to your last day, for there is no end to memory.

And memory is never still. Memory we fashion so that it will tell us what we think we wish to know. From one day to another there may be a difference in what that will be.

More than that, when you look at your memory what you see is not quite yourself, for you are more than your memory. You are all that you have been and could be. You may never, in your memory, see the true you. You are another—and many more than one. Your head is the home of difference. What does it take to see yourself as you are?

You pray for the time when you are one, when all that you are is composed to make the one you.

As for me, I know that time will come, and I will be in it and it will be in me. It may be that this is how I will know the right path when it comes: that I will then think and do, and it will be the one me that does so.

Then one day she was gone. She went in the night, and in the morning we had a home again.

I go down before my father and my brother for some reason. I look at the things I know so well: the door, the table, the window. But they do not seem as they did before: it's as if they have something to tell me. All is still.

How do I know she's gone? I cannot remember. But I *do know*. It comes to me right away.

She's gone. This is my home now. This is my father's home and my brother's home. This is home. I go up again to where they still are. Let the sun come in at my window! Let a robin sing! Before I could not truly wish for such things. Before was another day. Before is over.

I go down and lay the table.

My father did not tell us where she had gone: did he know? So in a way it was as if she had never been. We—my brother and I, that is—went on as we had. We did not think we should ask what had gone on, and I truly did not mind if I did not lay eyes on the lady again.

But that was not so for my brother, and when some time had gone by he would ask me where she could be now. I would make things up for him (it was my hope he could be turned from such thoughts, but this may not have been the way to do it), and he would make them up for himself. It was like play—but with something more to it.

'You will not see May-May again but I will,' he would say—most of all when I was in his way.

'She lost them, the eyes she had—remember how they would look at you? She went out to look for them, bended over, with a hand on the ground. She never could find them. She went on and on, day and night—for what is night to one with no eyes? And still she goes on, one hand on the ground, and the clothes she had on when she left are now all fouled. No-one will speak to such a one as she is.'

'She *does* love me. She will call me when she is here again.'

'She took up with that young soldier, but then lost him to another. She's lost all memory of us.'

'She is in heaven, with God, but will come to see me again and give me all I like.'

'She was in the chorus of a play, and now she's a lady of the night. Each day she becomes another, and each day is worse than the last.'

'She will remember me and give me a sweet when she comes, I know.'

'I know: she's the king's lady. That's it. She went to the king. She took over from the one that was there. She's with the king. Each day, almost, we see each other, and do not know it.'

8

Him—let me speak now of him: the young lord.

Now that I come to think of it, I cannot see what reason I could have had not to do this before, for he was there all the time, with my brother and me—with us each day, almost, from when he was little. It's not as if I have lost my memory of that—of him. How could I have? No, it's more that he was such a feature, being there with us, that he's never but in my thoughts as I remember. He's like the grass and the mountain.

Well no, he's not. I have to say it's not been like that with him for quite some time now. He's here still, indeed, but in a way, it's as if he's *not* here. You have turned to speak to him: you have him in your eyes, and his eyes seem to be on you—you think so—but it's as if his mind is on something quite other. He's lost to you. And it will go on like that when he comes to speak. It's as if his mind is two: one to speak, to look at you, to be with you, and one not. And it's been like this from long before the king his father died.

I know there are some that think his father's death made a difference to him, that he was all right before that. But believe me, he was not.

Still, there was a time when he was not so hard to be with: I have to remember that. And it's not that he's *hard* to be with now. It's more this, that it's not the way it was—not for me, and, no doubt, not for him. I believe that's so. All that is hard for me now—and each day becomes more so—is to know what goes on in his head.

No, again, 'hard' is not right. It's not hard. Nothing's hard with him. I love him still—as a brother, let me say—and I love being with him still.

Be that as it may, it's true that we do not have now what we had before, he and I—and my brother with us as well: the Thorny Thrice, as my little brother would call us then.

So let me go right away to that time long before this, that better time when he was young and so was I.

With a king for his father, he did not have so many they would think it right for him to play with. We had that honour—if honour it was. It could seem, at the time, more like something you did on command—to him as well, for he would tell me so.

They may not have meant to make it seem like something he had to do, but so it was. He had to wear his play-clothes. He had to have a steward to take him to us. He had to be observed all the time. Then they would take him home. That was the way of things.

If we went to where *he* was, it was worse. You could not take a breath without one of the ladies —two we had to mind us—would look up and say something. You could not go out to find saint's bells without the two of them would come with you.

One day we all went out like that, and then, at a look from him, I turned to go in again, and he went like all hell up the steep path to the mountain, and.... What did my brother do? Stayed still, that was it. That made them give us another lady to be with us all the time from then on, one each.

All this was so that he would know his difference from us, right from when he was little. They did what they could to take the joy away.

And we—we had to find what joy we could, find what we could say and could not say, with their eyes on us.

That made us the more close. It was us and them.

It was that way all the long months of his youth and mine, the months when the sun stayed where it was, and it would seem in the morning that the day would never end. He would come, with his wretched steward and the ladies. Most of the time it was for the day, but now and again he stayed over, and the steward would be in my brother's chamber, whilst the ladies went home for the night. As for us, we would all be in my bed (for they would let us do that, being all so little at the time), and we would speak of this and that. If not, we would be quite still and look out of the window as the day went. Many a time I turned to him, to see his eyes.

What I could *not* see then, but remember now, is that he would seem to find with us something he could not find at home.

No, that's not quite true. He did not *find* it, not with us. But with us he could *look*.

Now, as I think of that time, one memory falls over another, and what's left to me are remembrances all gyved and jangled. I have to keep one from another, keep now from then. I have to keep to the time we had before he would, little by little, close himself up to me—and, it may be, to himself. I have to think of that time before he went away from me, little by little, like the end of the day.

Do I have to say that he had, when he was at his own home, all he could wish for? That was all well and good, but it would have been better if I could have been there more of the time. If I was not, and my brother was not, he had no-one to speak with, play with, be with. All he had was things. And I think he would come to think of himself as one of these things. He was left more and more out of tune with himself.

This is not something that time will help. No, it becomes worse and worse. And it did so. I could see that. Young as I was, I would ask him what I could do to help, when he was with us but seemed out of it—as many a day he did. But he could not tell me.

If I say he would seem 'not himself', that's not quite right. Before long, being 'not himself' was how he was. There was no ground to him. And I had to take him as he was—if still hope that one day he would find help.

It was not that he lost his love for his father, not at all. That love was unmatched, and was more, I think, than his father's love for him. If he still rains love on his father now, with his father gone, so he did then. And from his father love rained so little. His father was not unkind, not that. But the late king did not know how to be a father—did not know that one had to be a father, that this was something one had to *do*. The king was the king. What should the king be more? To us, my brother and I, the king could show some affection, a little. But not to him.

I see him now, the king as was, in my mind's eye. Must I remember? It's hard to think it's been no more than two months, two little months.

When I was at the grave that cold morning —with my father and my brother, all of us as one, which by then was not the way of it most of the time—I had columbines in my hand. We could not sing (we did not know there would never be music again); we could not weep.

He had to be at the other end from us, by himself, his clothes done up to keep out the rains, his eyes down on the violets in *his* hand. We all had flowers that day.

The day before, when his father had died, he

had come right away to be with us—this time it was *not* something they made him do—and he had stayed the night, as long before. Now he could have his own bed, which had been the maid's.

One night was all it was. Then his time with us was over—for good, it seemed. We did not know if he would have things to do for the state. As it turned out, he did not. But he did have to be on hand.

And now here he was, at the other end of the grave. And *he* could not weep.

As we left, some of the ladies turned to one another to say they could not make him out. What reason could he have not to weep, given his love for his father? Was it that he did not wish to make a show? Was it that he held himself in, did not let go, so that he could do what he had to do?

He observed all there was to be observed. He would look at me from time to time, as we all turned to the grave to pray. There was nothing in his eyes.

I go again to what he was like when he was little.

When he would come to play, the maid would take us all up the mountain, and then at length we would come down again, with the sun. And

his steward would be a little way away. (No ladies: this was before we had to have them with us as well.) For that steward it must have been such a bore. But we had no thoughts for the steward.

If it rained we stayed in. That he seemed to like more, and as for us, we did not mind. The maid would tell us things by heart, of the Snow King, the Lady and the Rose, the Green Men, and such. And he would love this. He would be quite still and composed, in his play-shirt. I would look at him, and it seemed that the words meant more to him than they did to us, to me. It seemed as if I could see what they meant to him from the look in his eyes, from how he held himself. It was almost as if I could keep up with the words that way, and close my mind to the maid. I would look at him as he sucked up the words and what was in them, and it would please me that we could do this for him: there was so little we could.

This was all—I do not have to say—long before he went away to be a scholar. This was when there was nothing to keep him from us. If we did not see him one day, we would know they would have him with us tomorrow. Tomorrow we would be with one another again.

But by the time he went away it was not like it

had been. He would still come. But he would speak as little as he could, and think before he did so. Two words from him was a speech. There had been a time when he was as close to me as my own heart. Now he was not. Now he held me at arm's length. No. It was something other than him, something that held him as well as me, the two of us at arm's length from each other.

I do not know what it was, but he had gone from me. He would go more. He was a youth now, and not a youth you could know well.

Then again, I could see now that I never *did* know him, not truly know him. The young do not know the young. But they see and they remember. A little of what he had been was in him still, for me. That little I held on to. And he was still in my thoughts all the time. He is so now, more than most.

But when I think of him, I think of all I do not know. For some time now he's given away so little of himself that I would have to say 'I think him' more than 'I know him'. I have him in my thoughts—and in my memory.

I wish he could know that. I wish I could tell him. I wish I could find the words to tell him. But I cannot. In these last months I have seen him more again. He'll come to me and ask me, his eyes locked on me as he does so, to think of him—not pray for him, but think of him, think *with* him—and to tell him that I do so, and that I will do so, for as long as it will take. Each time I have promised. Each time I tell him I *do* think of him, all the time; he does not have to ask. And he will cast his eyes away from me and go.

Another time he'll come to me and do no more than look at me, his eyes hard on mine. One day, when he was like this, I had to say something. Did he think I was the one with the answers? Did he think I, like them, would keep things from him, make him believe things are other than they are? Before I had done I could see this was not the way to go on. Now I know what to do: keep still, no words.

There's something he must have from me, and he cannot tell me what it is. If he could tell me, I would give it. But it may be that to tell me would be to have it lost. That would be the end. So by the look on his face he'll ask and ask and ask—for more each time, it will seem. And I know that nothing I could say would be right.

There was a time when I would hope that one day I could know what to say—could come up with it, and all this would be over. But that hope's gone. I do not know—and I know I'll never know—what it is he must have from me. I do not have that access to his mind I did have; I cannot be in there with him. All I may do is have him here in mine.

I have him here now, from another day long gone, when he had come to be with us for some time. My brother was away with Gis, which meant he could take over my brother's bed, and they did not think he had to have a steward with him now, and we had lost the ladies for good, and my father was most of the time in bed with some speech. She? She had gone, not so long before. So it was we two. And still at this time there was nothing he had to keep from me. We could truly be as one.

We would be up with the sun each morning. We had no lesson to keep us in, and so we would go over the mountain to see the holy men and play the bells, then take the path to Long Wheel, where there's what's left of a grave-ground from before the Christian time, then come home again.

All day long we would speak—and again at night, and almost to morning, with me in my bed and him over there, his shoulders upon the door of the closet—and speak of many things: of memory and how it is that we remember, of if there is an end to reason and if that is where you find God (this was all at a time when we would think of such things), of some poll the state took (and he would be shaking his head), of being and non-being, of words and things, of his state of doubt.

We could still, then, speak from the heart. The words would go on and on as if we did not have to think what to say.

Now it's not like that at all. Now I'll say something, and I'll look at him, and he'll have his head down, his hand over his eyes. If not that, then he'll go on with some argument, on and on, whilst I'll be left with nothing to say, and indeed there'll be nothing to say, for in the end, in all these words, he'll keep his own counsel. It'll be as if the words had not been his—as if it had all been in play, but with no joy to it. He'll be a speech without a face. And how may I speak to that?

When he's gone I'll think what it all meant. It could be there was something he would like to say—something he almost *had* to say, and would come close to, something that was right at the end of his tongue, but then he held it in. The steward was gone: he was now—this is how it's come to seem to me—his own watchman. He observed himself.

He's done this for a good long time—observed himself and observed the one he's with, to see what effect he'll have. We all do this when we are young, but with him it's gone on. And they have not seen it.

But I have. And I see it now, more and more. Does he fear he could give himself away? With me? If so, he does not know me at all. And if *that's* so, I indeed do not know him.

I cannot find the key to him. There was a time when I would look for it. Then I did not look.

That made no difference to him. He's not lost this wish to have me with him all the time, as if all is still as it was. But he'll have nothing to say to me, no more than this play of words. I do not mind that we speak so little of me, for that's something I never did hope for. All I wish is that it could be other than it is. I wish he could have more joy in himself: that would be something. It is not to be.

What he *will* say, now and again, is that there's no other he may be himself with. But that's not true. Most of what's himself is locked away from me, and it's been that way for a long time. It could be that it's locked away from him, as well. Does he still know what it means: to be himself?

But it means something to my father that I'll be there when he comes, that I'll have stayed with him for as long as he'll wish, that I'll never have something better to do. Of that I have no doubt: you see it in my father's eyes.

When he comes to the door, my father will go to let him in, and then close the door and look at him, as if to say: 'At last!' Never mind if we have seen him the day before, and the day before that.

Did they ask my father to do this for them? Did he take it on himself? That would be so like him: to see something that *had* to be done, and to do it—to give himself, and his daughter, over to their wish. No, not to their wish, but to what had to be done for them, and they did not know it, could not see it. That being so, they would never thank him. And for my father it would be better that way.

So that'll give me something, that I may please my father in that I please him—if please him is what I do. If I have long given up hope that one day I would come to know him, still more have I lost all expectation of something from him. That I know I'll never receive. Now he's a way to please my father. That's most of it. He's a way to give my father joy when so little will. And how could I have denied my father?

Up to the time the king died we would play music—the bells, as before, but other things as well, at home. (My brother by now had his own music he was in to, and had gone from the music chamber, given me the key.) He would love to have me sing to him, and for that reason I would love to do so. Now I may do no more than say the words, the words he would ask me to sing.

> *The bonny soldier now is dead,*
> *Violets he bore me.*
> *I will cast them on my bed,*
> *Let it in his grave be.*

But this is something from another time. Without music it means nothing. Without music it could make me fear.

There are other young men here I could be with. There was a time when two from over the way would come to ask me out with them and another 'young lady': that's how they would speak. But I could not go. What if he should come and find me gone? How could I have a good time with them like that? Now they have given me up.

So there are things I have lost, things I could have had but did not, which is all right, being as it's all for my father. But I have to say it does not make me like *him* more.

I love him. I cannot but love him. Love is not like.

It's been hard, indeed hard, to keep it up, day upon day. Without my father to think of I would not have done so.

As for him, what was his reason? What could be the end of it all? Still, he would come in the morning—never mind if we had been up late the night before—and I could not say no to him.

To speak truly, it's not all for my father. There's been the hope as well, right up to now, that I could do more for *him*, that there would come the day when we could speak to each other as we did when young—no, speak as we had never done before. And that hope's still not quite left me.

It almost went one day, not long before the king's death, when we had gone up the mountain. There was something I had to ask him: I could not go on with these thoughts and say nothing.

So I did ask. It was to do with love, true love. It had to do with me and another. But it was as if I had importuned him: he turned to me with such a look in his eyes that I did not know what to do. Did I say something I should not have? What had I done? What had I lost? It seemed to me, there and then, that now we could never be close again as we had been, that now he could never show himself. It was all over. And I was to blame. We went down.

For some months I had no wish to be with him, and no wish to be without him. He had made me without wish.

I was cold. I could not speak to him. Then I could—but of other things. And before I could quite know it, my heart bore again the wish and the hope.

As for him, I see him now as one that does not have that wish and that hope—does not know what wish and hope are. They took these things from him, a little at a time. And how could I restore them? I could not.

He goes on. But there's no path that he's on. He goes this way and that.

This will make him seem cold—and he is,

indeed, that: out in the cold. But, take him for all in all, he's cold without the wish to be so. He's without wish. He's without will.

All we could make, over time, was a way of being with each other. It's little help to us, I know. I do not like it. He does not like it. But it's what we have.

I have turned these things over in my mind, again and again, as if that would make a difference—as if I could see my remembrances another way, see that things have all the time been other than I think. But they have not.

There are some, I know, that think they know him better than I do, and it may be they do. But I doubt it. And then there are some that come to me as if I should be the one to tell them what they wish to know. 'Does he think it'll be better for the state if the mark falls?', they'll say. 'What clothes should I wear?' 'How's he on fennel?' 'Do you think he would like a Bells?' 'Will he give more to charity when he's king?' 'Is a little perfume all right, given that it'll be morning?' 'Does he have a death wish?' Not to speak of my brother, with his: 'What's he like in bed?'

How could they think I know? I look at them. They go away and say there's no hope for me, my tongue is not my own. If not that, they make up things. Well, let them. I cannot tell another what's so tumbled in my own mind.

I cannot say—as little as this—what he's like to one that's not seen him. Are his eyes green? It may be they are; I cannot remember. And it's not that there's nothing in his countenance you would have lost your head over, not at all. Many have done: men as well. Some still do.

That's up to them. He never had such an effect on me, being as close to me as a brother when he was little. And it's not true that my father had the hope he *would*: my father would never wish for you what you did not and could not wish for yourself.

It may not have been so with the king as was. And I think the king's lady may still have such thoughts. But if so, she will have to think again. How should I be wed to one I know I cannot know? There never was a hope of that with him and me, and there never will be. That's all I have to say on that one.

Some think they know better: my brother for one, as well as other young men that may have been deceived. I know my brother loosed his tongue here and there. But let them have their way. What they have to say means nothing to me, being such a long way from what's true. I have denied it. Still they go on. So what?

I go on with my thoughts—and it may be I think more than I should. There was a time when my father would say that to me, and say that no good would come of it. But my father could not have meant that. It was my father that *made* us think, my brother and me. That was something my father did make us do. I cannot now say: 'Let me not think'.

And indeed, as I now think, there are some things I may say of him and not doubt right away if it's so. Here's one: how he'll love it when we go to a play, and love it still more to be *in* a play. Make-believe is his one true joy.

I remember by heart one play we did, and I'll come to that. As for what it's like to be with him at a play, I have to say this: it's hard to make him keep still. He'll see himself in the play—as a lord that's given away all he had, a young soldier-king with his sword raised, one that's made an oath in expectation of imports he does not receive, one so in love with a lord's daughter that he bore on his shoulders what the father would ask. He'll be there, in the play. He'll call out; he'll weep. And all for nothing: for a play. One cannot but think: what would he do had he good reason?

I wish he would not do this, and I ask him not to, but it'll make no difference. It's something more than him. It'll almost make me fear, to see him like this, how a play will take him over.

Most of the time that's how it is, but now and again he'll be left cold by a play, and that's worse, for then he'll have to tell me his thoughts and ask me mine. In that way we almost make *another* play, a play upon the play. And as my answers are never right for him, he'll have to say more, ask me more, tell me more what I should think. There's no end to it, for when the play's come to an end, then this other play, of him and me, will go on, and we'll still be in *that* play by the time we have come home.

There may be more to this. It may be that the play truly never does end, that it goes on and on. He'll play himself, and what must I play? Himself as well. He'll take me over, as one in a play took him. He would play upon me. I have to show him what he is. Without me—indeed, without all of us—he's nothing. And we—we are nothing but him. In this play of his we all have to be him. He may see nothing but himself, as if each of us is a glass to him. That it should come to this! This is his hell, and we are with him there.

9

I come, as promised, to a play we all did—him, my brother, my father and me, we being all the cast. Like him, I love being in a play, most of all for the months before you do it, when you have to remember your words, speak them over and over with each other, find more and more what the play means. The play is not still: it becomes something. Then comes the time when you have your clothes for the show, and you all look at one another, and see each other another way. There's a difference, as well, in how you see yourself. You have lost yourself, to find yourself again in the play.

Before that, when you still do not know the words by heart, it's better to be at a table, all of you. Then you may think of how you should say the words, and of no more than that—not of where you should be and what you should do.

If these other things come up, you may make a mark in long hand.

My brother would take it on himself to be the one to tell us what to do, and on this one day I well remember he was there at the table, with the play in his hand, from which he did not look up to see my father and me come in.

MY BROTHER: Good to see you.

Which he could not—but which he had to say to show how little he meant it.

MY FATHER/ME: Good to see *you*.
MY BROTHER: Could you give me a hand and
                be here when I ask? Thank you.

He still had his eyes on the play, not on us.

MY FATHER: Better late than never!

At this he did at last look up.

MY BROTHER: *I* would like it more if you could
                be here when I say. So would you
                keep that in mind from now on?
                As you may see, *he's* here.

As indeed *he* was. He had raised himself from the table as we had come in, and we had cast a look at one another whilst my brother stayed with his head in the play.

MY BROTHER: If he may be here by one, so may you.

He was waving a hand now to show where we should be: me on his left, my father at the end of the table.

ME: Hey ho, here we go again....

He went on.

MY BROTHER: Now that you *are* all here, let's give this a go. Father mine would you do Denmark for now? Thank you. You all know where you are? So: on with it!

MY FATHER: *Did you call, madam?*

MY BROTHER: No. Could you, may be, give it some more—like so's one could believe in you a little? Do you think? Thank you.

MY FATHER: *Did you call, madam?*

MY BROTHER: More!
MY FATHER: *Did you call, madam?*
MY BROTHER: That's not it, but go on.
ME: *Thank you, Denmark. Would you
              be so good as to take the young
              master's hat up to him?*

I cannot remember now what this play was. We
had done *All's Well That End's Well* before this,
and what a night that had been—you would not
believe!—on the mountain as the sun went down.

MY FATHER: *Indeed, madam.*
ME: *By the way, Denmark, this is his
              lordship's hat, is it not?*
MY FATHER: *I believe so, Your Grace.*
ME: *Thank you, Denmark, that will
              be all.*

I was the young lord's lady in this play. (Well,
that's the way it goes: I could have had to make
love to my brother, which would have been
worse.) And he's a help. He's a reckless way with
him when you are all in a play—quite a difference
from how he is as himself.

MY FATHER: *Indeed, Your Grace.*

MY BROTHER: May he say this as if he means it, do
          you think?
MY FATHER: *Indeed, Your Grace.*
MY BROTHER: So go on then: do it.
MY FATHER: That *was* it: 'Indeed, Your Grace'.
MY BROTHER: Never mind. Go on, 'Your Grace'.
HIM: *There, Rose, what did I tell you?*
            Denmark is in on this.
MY BROTHER: Well done: good affection on the
            'Rose'. Thank you. Now you
            again, O.
ME: *In on what, Do-Do?*
MY BROTHER: No, not 'do, do'. It's 'Do-Do'—you
            know: 'Dead as a Do-Do'.
ME: Right you are. *In on what, Do-Do?*

The young lord did not seem to know he should
come in here.

MY BROTHER: Go on, there's a love.
HIM: *In on how To-To must have*
            deceived the baker's daughter,
            that's all!
ME: *I cannot think, Do-Do, that To-To*
            would have Denmark know of his
            —. O, there you are, To-To. Did
            Denmark find you with your hat?

MY BROTHER:	*Indeed. That was what made me come here.*
ME:	*My true, true To-To. You know my way.*
MY BROTHER:	I may not like it, but I do know it.
ME:	Hey, that's not in the play!
MY BROTHER:	I know. Go on.
MY FATHER:	I do not know at all where we are now.
MY BROTHER:	You are not on. Remember? O: 'Now I must go—'
ME:	*Now I must go and have a little heart to heart with Joy.*
HIM:	*When you fair things have some-thing you must tell one another heart to heart, what you will speak of will be men!*
ME:	*To speak thus, Do-Do, becomes you not at all. Mark me, to be merry you would have to be profound.* When do I come on again?
MY BROTHER:	If that means may you go now, no.
HIM:	*Fare you well, my love. But To-To, tell me, what is all this with Grace?*
MY BROTHER:	I think there should be more here, you know? Would he come out with it like that?

ME:	No way! What do *you* think father?
MY FATHER:	Indeed, madam.
MY BROTHER:	Thank you, O. It may be I'll have to give him some more here. Another speech? I'll think.
ME:	It's your call.
MY BROTHER:	But let's go on with it for now. *Grace? I know no Grace. Would that I could! I know I would have to love one I could call 'Grace'.*
MY FATHER:	*Lord Rich is here, Your Grace.*
HIM:	*O, show him in, Denmark, show him in, there's a good—*
MY FATHER:	*Do-Do! I say!*

I remember how the play went when we did it: so well. My father stole the show as Lord Rich. He did it all with his eyes: the look of expectation, then of doubt when Do-Do would not tell him what he had come for. All of that he had right away.

HIM:	*Be-Be! My, my!*
MY FATHER:	*You see? I turned up on time!*
HIM:	*So it would seem!*
MY BROTHER:	*For what?*

MY FATHER:	*To find you here, To-To—and good it is to see you!*
MY BROTHER:	*And you, my lord. How goes it with you, may I ask?*
MY FATHER:	*So so, To-to, so so. But I know you fare better, is that not so?*
MY BROTHER:	*You may say so, my lord. There are some as do not.*
MY FATHER:	*Ecstasy, ecstasy! But do please call me 'Be-Be'.*
HIM:	*We may let form go here, I should hope!*
MY BROTHER:	*So we may, father. Thank you, Be—*
ME:	*Be-Be! I do wish Denmark would tell me when you are here! I had to see to the pansies with Joy, but I do not like to be denied you!*
MY FATHER:	*The lady of the May, as we know and love!*
ME:	*Be-Be, sweet! Did To-To tell you Bonny and Noble did indeed take him on? As of now what he will make there is quite little, but he should do well in time to come.*
MY FATHER:	*If he does not find a lady of means!*
ME:	*The young do not wed, Be-Be. They have left it to us, to wed twice.* know

MY BROTHER:	*May-May!*
ME:	Does he say 'May-May'?
MY BROTHER:	He does now. Do you mind?
ME:	I do, but go on.
MY BROTHER:	*For shame!*
ME:	*There is no shame, To-To, when one does well in imports: charity, I believe, should end at home. But let me look at you, To-To. I must say I like that shirt you have on. Where did it come from?*
MY BROTHER:	*My brother.*
ME:	*So like him. Young men should believe in nothing but the clothes they wear.*

My brother did To-To in his own shirt.

HIM:	*I fear there may be something other than fashion for young men to believe in, my sweet.*
ME:	*Indeed? And what would that be, Do-Do?*
HIM:	*Love.*
MY FATHER:	*Do-Do, you speak like a green youth! Madam, I blame this on you! What did you do to make such a being in*

	your own home?
ME:	*I cannot now remember, Be-Be. I keep Denmark as my memory and my daughter to tell me my mind.*
MY FATHER:	*Indeed, that is what a daughter is for.* Did we cast the daughter?
MY BROTHER:	No, but I will. Go on.
MY FATHER:	*But tell me, how is Go-Go?*
ME:	*My brother's daughter? I wish I did not have to remember: wed to a scholar—I ask you! One of these young men that know more words than God but will say nothing when they are at your table.*
MY FATHER:	*Poor show. Not like Do-Do here.*
HIM:	*I may speak of nothing, but I do so to good effect.*
MY BROTHER:	I think I should be the one to say that.
ME:	Well, you are not.
MY BROTHER:	I'll see to that, if you do not mind. But let's go on as it is for now.
MY FATHER:	*Now, To-To!*
MY BROTHER:	Could you *not* come in before you should?
MY FATHER:	But I was—
MY BROTHER:	*Father!*

MY FATHER:	*Now, To-To!*
MY BROTHER:	*I know: 'Honour thy father that he may remember you in his will.'*
MY FATHER:	*Indeed. But keep this in mind as well, To-To: never mind what your father may say, you should keep 'love' as the last of the words you speak, for as to effect, we may never know what effect that, of all words, will have!*
HIM:	*Be-Be, you speak truly—and indeed, one such effect is what we meant to speak of when you—*
ME:	*My sweet, I doubt that Be-Be will have come here so that we may tell him such things—not, most of all, before Denmark. Denmark!*
MY FATHER:	*Madam.*
ME:	*Pray see if there is some fennel we could have.*
MY FATHER:	*I shall do so, madam. What a find you have there!*
ME:	No father, that's Be-Be.
MY BROTHER:	He *is* Be-Be as well as Denmark, remember?
ME:	Indeed. Right. *The letters had nothing to do with it!*

MY BROTHER: What?

ME: O, I turned over before I should.

MY BROTHER: I give up!

ME: *To-To! Now that I look at you*
again, what means this state of your
heels?

MY BROTHER: *I lost another one, May-May.*

ME: Do you *have* to go on like this?

MY BROTHER: *I lost another one, May-May.*

ME: *To have lost one sandal, To-To, may*
look piteous. To have lost the two
will seem like dalliance.

10

Then there would be the morning when I had to go up the mountain and take no-one with me, up to the brow where all is green and you seem to be at the door to the heavens. That's where I go to pray, when I *do* pray, in my own words, to the God I know to have gone from us—but still I pray.

O God, what was your reason? How may I pray to you now that you have left us? You made us and you stayed, and it must have been good to know that you would be there, and would keep an eye, like a sun in the heavens, to make it day all the time. Now there is no eye on us, and the night goes on without end.

O Lord, you have gone; And are with us no more. This is not what you promised, to the one that went up to see you on the mountain; He that held in his hand the things of your command you should not have deceived.

We had come to think you would last to the time when there was time no more; We had come to believe that you, like no other being, held in yourself the powers to be.

But you left like an owl in the night; O God, when you went, we could see no mark in the grass.

How without you could it be that the sun rises; How could each herb go on being green?

How was the sweet rose to give his perfume again; And the thorny rose to keep his beauty?

If God is no more with us, I pray to what is, be it so little. I pray to the pansies as I do to the morning; I pray to memory and the wheel of time. And I pray to the day when God was; and I pray to the nothing where God was. That nothing: I cannot keep it in my mind. If I do so, it becomes something. It goes away. O nothing, you are so like God, for you, as well, have gone from us.

There was another come from God to say: God is dead.

O Father that is not in heaven, is heaven still there? Does mercy have a home? And is there ground for hope? Are charity and honour now no more than words? Is there still, to close over us, the heart of love?

11

My brother, by now, I had to think of as one of the men: he had a little beard. That made quite a difference to how we would be with one another. Each morning now he stayed in bed late—if, that is, he had come home at all the night before. And I would never see him before he was up and in his clothes: that time we had had, morning upon morning, to tell each other things in bed was all over. Then he would go out—most of the time with two other young things. He would not tell us where they went, what they did.

One of them would come to call for him: I would know it was one of them from the hard knocking, twice.

'I'll go', my brother would say.

'Yield!', the one at the door would say. It could be more like ' 'ild', if not 'dild'.

'I do so!'—this from my brother. And then from the two of them: 'One for all and all for one!' I believe there was some way they had of hand-shaking now, but they would not let us see. What it all meant my brother never did say—not that we would ask. It seemed to be more for us than for them: a way to keep us locked out from what they did.

Then they would go, still with nothing to say to us. My father would look up as my brother went to the door, then, when the two of them had left, go on as before.

That's how my brother was. My father would keep out of his way—indeed, they did not speak to each other if he, my brother, could help it. That was one reason my father had such joy in his eyes when he was in a play with my brother, for then my brother would *have* to speak to him, which was better than nothing.

As for my brother and me, we would speak to each other from time to time, but there was something a little false in how we did so. It may be it would have been better if we could have been a little more unkind, a little more ungracious with each other, as we had before. Now I would look at him, but he could not look at me.

If my eyes would come upon his, he would look away.

I remember the mark this made on me one day, with all of us still at the table, late in the morning: my brother, my father and I. We have another maid now, but she's not there: she's made something for us and left for the day.

My father rises from the table and goes, for he would know that my brother will not speak—if the young cockle should wish to speak at all—whilst he's there. That's how it is. Never does my father ask me what my brother had to say, never. Never does he ask for answers from my brother. He's left my brother to me; he'll take what comes for a time, and hope for more.

On many a morning what my brother had to say would be nothing at all: how it had rained in the night, what did I think of his hat. But there would be something more as well. In all he would speak, something other was meant. And I know where this had come from.

There had been a time, long before, when we did such two-time speech in play.

'Let's play Quoth.'

'My go then. You tell me what I have to say and how I have to say it.'

'Say "Come what may" so that it means "Death to you that denied a soldier's honour!"'

'Come what may!'

'Ha ha! My go.'

But now it seemed we did this all the time.

As for that morning, my father had been gone for as long as it took my brother to find his grass. Then he turned to look at me.

'That fashion does nothing for your bulk, you know.' And he took his eyes away. He took another draw, and again turned to me, with something harsh in his look.

'What would you like me to say?'

'Say what you will.'

'No, you tell me. I have no will.'

'Right, I'll ask this, again. Where did you go last night?'

'Out.'

'With?'

'What do you think? The Violets.' That's what they would call each other. I should have left it at that, but I went on.

'What did you do?' And here, all at one go, he loosed his hand from the table and bore his face right down at mine. His hope, I think, was to give me a look that could have withered the soul.

'Death! Death! Death!'

What should I have done now? I believe I made him think it was hard for me to keep composed, as in a way it was. I stayed where I was, my eyes on his. He had on the pale make-up they would all wear, these 'Violets', and the grass was on his breath. He stayed with his face close to mine for as long as it would take me to say twice over: 'Remember he's your brother.' And still I did nothing but keep my eyes on his. Then there was a hand on my right shoulder, as if to say this was all over now, and he took himself away. I turned to see the door close.

It did not go on for long like that, with him out each night. But it seemed long at the time. Then one day there was no more knocking, no more words at the door, no more hand-shaking we could not see, no more not being in bed before two in the morning if then, no more pale make-up and no more Violets. Now my brother would speak to my father again, and my father would ask me—I remember twice when he did so— what I had done to restore 'Little' to him (by now it may not have been a help to call him that). I had to say I had done nothing, which was true. But I doubt my father could quite believe it: he would look at me with 'I know there's more to this' in his eyes, and then speak of other things. He had my brother again: his head and his hand if not his heart. He did not have to know the reason.

What I could never say to my father—could say to no-one—was that there was a reason for how my brother now was, and that the reason was love. If he could but look, my father would see it. Young 'Little' bore himself better. Clothes meant more to him, and before he went out for the night (which he still did, but not so late) he would take a brief look at himself in the glass by the door, to see the effect he made. Then he would sing as he left—not the harsh music of the Violets, music no-one could sing, but something sweet and touching from my father's day. You could see how my father would like that.

We still did not know where he went. And I never did find out which young madam it was (there are not so many it could have been) that had given my brother a shoulder on which to lay that head of his—that head he had lost. But whilst I would never think to ask, he did let me in on his joy in a way.

Letters would come for him each morning, and some of them—not all—he would let me see. But he would say nothing, and I was to say nothing. I did not know the hand, but I do remember some of these letters well, for the lady had a way with words.

What's mine is yours and what is yours is mine,
But should I give you what was mine before?
The sweet remembrance of a libertine
Becomes, if one would tell it, quite a bore.
Let me not say, then, how some soldier's hand
Would find each night a touching way to please,
How this could make it last all morning and
That redeliver keen upon his knees.
One I remember comes to me in bed
And comes again twice more before he goes.
There was a scholar: how I held his head!
And how he sucked the perfume from my rose!
*   You now, and then I'll take another he,*
*   For difference means more than length to me.*

Now that my father could speak to my brother again, they could be seen with each other all over: on the green, by the falls, up the mountain, one of them with a speech of my father's in his hand. I think my father did not know quite what to make of it, and had no wish to ask.

It was a joy to me to see them with each other. I did not mind at all if this meant I was left out a little. And each of them would still wish to be with me from time to time. Never (so I believe) did my father see my brother's love letters, and never would my brother come to know what my father now and again would say to me—things to do with the state of his soul, for there was a memory he would go over again and again, tell me again and again, of how he had deceived the king-as-was so as to receive something promised by the king-as-would-be.

And there was another reason I did not mind if I was a little away from my father and my brother at this time, for I had—I may say this now—a love of my own. I did not speak of that to my brother. He had other things on his mind.

> *I cannot tell what you and other men*
> *Have done before to give me such a lay*
> *And make me think then's now and now is then:*
> *You did as they—you took my breath away.*
> *My powers of speech went when you took*
>   *my breath;*
> *My tongue had other things to do than tell.*
> *You give me love and in this give me death:*
> *I cannot say but sigh—I hope sigh well.*
> *My mind is down. My mind is blown,*
>   *o'erthrown.*

Then letters form again: they come from you,
As we make love and make words that we own,
To say all we may say in what we do.
    The sun is gone. Come to me now. It's late.
    The love that cannot speak by love we state.

My brother had one of his letters in his hand one
morning—down at the table, with my father still
in bed with a speech—when he turned to speak
to me.

'Do you think I do as I like?'

'Which means...?'

'Is it indeed *I* that does things? Do I tell me
where to go, when to go in, when to go out? Is
there not another I, one I do not know, but that
is in me, and it will have me do things? I do not
know if I may, here and now, tell you what I will
with my own mind, the mind I know.'

'You may and you are. This is what "you" are:
you are what you do and what you say, and you
are all you do and all you say. There's no other in
there with you—but indeed, you may have an
argument with yourself.'

'How if it's like this, that what you are—what
was you up to now, the you that you know—is
not what you long to be?'

I did not know quite what to say.

'It may seem like that, indeed it may. There are, let us say, things that are given us, that are some of what we are. They may be hard for us to keep down, so that we may do as we wish.'

'And where could they come from, these things?'

'Look up there out of the window. You see? The way you raised an arm over your eyes when you had to look at the sun: that comes from father, you know. I do it as well, now and again.'

'So there are things I do that are *not* mine, and that's one of them, as it is for you. I *have* to do it. It goes on in my head and I do not know it's there. It's not me.'

'O but it is! There are indeed things in yourself that you do not now know. In time you will find these things and make them yours. If not, you will cast them away. They may come again, but you will know what to do. The "you" that you make, day by day, becomes more rich and more in command. Some things, no doubt, are hard to master, and with these you will have to find a way to draw them in to yourself, so that they cannot take you over.'

'What if you long for them to take you, long to have no more say? What if all you are is in this state? What then?'

It is not night when I do see your face,
For with it comes the cock of morning's call:
The cock of ecstasy and cock of grace,
The cock of heaven and hell, the cock of all,
The cock that made me love and made me fear,
The cock of joy that could not be denied,
The cock to tell me what 'tis to be here,
The cock I would wish with me as I died.
Touching that cock my tongue a way may find
To honour him more than I honour some:
'Most beauteous cock', I'll say, and call to mind
How sweet that cock may make the honey come.
   You know this cock, my love, for it is yours:
   Yours to keep in, yours to let out of doors.

Each morning he would go to the door for the letters, and then come to the table again, his head down as he went over the words. Then he would go over them again, and again and again. There could be two such letters for him—more. Then, when my father had gone up, would be the time for him to show them to me.

One morning may go for many. He had gone to find the letters: two for him and one for me. I'll keep mine and look at it when I have more time. He'll tear in to his. Father's will come when the king's steward's men have had a look.

'Is she good to you?' I had to ask.
'She is.'
'And you: you are good to—'
'Have no fear.'
I had to say more, but what?
'You and I have not', I went on, 'been quite as—'
He raised a hand.

> *They do not love that do not show their love,*
> *So should this love we have go on not seen?*
> *You are my owl, my robin and my dove,*
> *You are what is to come and what hath been.*
> *I see you in the flowers upon the grass,*
> *I see you when I think and when I pray,*
> *I see you when I look in to a glass,*
> *I see you as the sun and as the day.*
> *You are my saint, so I in God believe;*
> *My soul is in your hand, yours not to blame:*
> *All that I ask is that you should receive*
> *These gifts in which there never could be shame.*
> > *In my heart as in yours there is no doubt:*
> > *What reason then, my love, not to come out?*

We went out and up the mountain, he and I.
He did not ask of me and my love. Never.
But he must see it. They must all see it.

12

O my honey, my love, o away up on the breath of a sigh we go, hey, as what is us rises in this light, out of the window and over the morning and over the day, and up steep to the light as the heels of heaven draw us, and us touching the sun with one hand, touching the light that is keen like joy on that one hand that comes from the two of us and we do not know which.

This is what it was, my heart, and this is what it will be.

As for now, I do not mind if it is day, if it is night.

Is the sun up? No. Then it must be night.

An owl will call to the night with grave music. A robin vows it is now morning, and bells the morning.

Night, day: there is no difference for me. What

will make the difference is if you are with me.

We have been with each other in the night and in the day. You would find me at night and speak to me of your day. I would find you in the morning and tell you of my night. We would be givers to each other, givers of night and day.

What will truly make it day for me is you. It is night now, for you are not here. This is true night, this is what it is, without you, that are my sun.

You are my sun. You have sun-blasted me, and turned me to light.

You have made me like glass—like glass in an ecstasy from your light, like glass in which light rained and rained and rained and goes on, like glass in which there are showers of light that cannot end.

It is as if my hand, my arm, my shoulder, all of me is nothing now but this light.

you are the sun
your two eyes are the doors of the sun
and it is mine to be blown from the sun
and it is mine to be sucked in to the sun
light in light

We are two souls in one. They should see this. They should fear me. They should not know what it is that they have before their eyes. Their eyes should be jangled by me, by you in me, by the sun in me.

What reason do they have, then, to say nothing to me? What reason do they have to go on as if this—this light-being, this being of light—could still be me as I was?

They should have raised an arm over their eyes. They should have held their eyes from me, turned from me, not to look at the sun that is in me.

How may they be at table with the sun?

How may they speak of what clothes to wear for the morning when they have with them showers of light?

You have made me this.

This is the reason there's no difference of day from night. In the night I see by my own light, which is your light. Light falls from me, your light. And it falls without end, as it comes to me from you without end.

But then you are, as well, night. You are the sun and you are night. You draw light to the in-most of you. You take in light and it goes.

When you are with me, it is as if we are in a night that we have made, a night that you and I have made for us, a home of night in the day.

It is as if, where we are, there could be no other light but what we are: this light of two as one.

You come to me, and I have to find my way to you with my hand, touching you with my hand, in the profound night of you.

My eyes still see, but what they see means nothing. Nothing they see is true. What is true cannot be seen, for all that is true we may say in two words: my love. And this all we may say in another two words: your love. There is no difference. My love is your love, as I and you are one—one in the night that is us. There is nothing but us. There is nothing but love.

What was, in all of time, was us and love. What will come we do not fear, for it will come and we will know it: us and love.

We will make light of that day when we are wed: it is no more than one tomorrow, and we have many. The bells and the flowers and the music and the vows: these are all nothing. These go. We last.

Your hand is in my hand. My heart is in your heart.

we have one heart
to keep and restore us

from here to tomorrow
we call that heart love

And I may call it us. Us. This little one of my words, king of my words.

I say it again and again: it is sweet on my tongue. Us. Us. Us. I have to have more and more of it, and I may make more and more of it, when I wish and where I wish. Us. Us.

Us. I have had this honey with me for months, on my tongue and in my mind. To be away from you would end me, so I have you with me night and day, on my tongue. You and I to make us. Us. Us. Us.

'I' and 'me', we may let them go: they are words we may do without. They could be lost, for what could they be to us when we are lost in each other?

If we look now, as this 'us' rises to the heavens, at the things that have been 'I' and 'me', what do we see? Things that long for you—things that do not know you are never away. Letters blown over and shaking, waving in the light of the sun that we now are. Letters lost in the night that we are.

From when we made us, these words meant nothing. I do not believe in them. I believe in us.

Come here. Be here again with me. When you come, we will be here again. You will restore us.

Remember how it was when we dove down the ecstasy of the heavens to be with one another. We will do that again.

Be with me shoulder to shoulder, arm in arm, as we face what we must face. Be with me touching me.

Do you remember when we lay down in the grass on the brow of the mountain? My face is in that grass now. No-one but you could find me here. And you will find me. We will be here again, in the grass and the flowers.

> *a hand touching a hand becomes a rose*
> *what the hand is touching becomes a rose*
> *rose on rose, rose in rose, rose and rose*
> *a rose that, shaking, rises as another rose*

I did not know what I was before. I did not know I was meant to be one of two. I was lost and did not know the reason. Now I know. I took the lesson from you. Two are better than one.

You are my path, and you are with me on that path, hand in hand, and you find your path in me. Each of us treads on the other, but so light.

I will be where you are, and if you are there, so

must I be. We cannot now be lost from each other.

And we are more. Look: we are a table, we are a green bed, we are a glass of violets at the window in the morning sun, we are a door out to the mountain, we are that mountain, we are all.

o green bed of green light
you loosed and composed me
your hand is a herb
your arm another
and these have held me as
I have gone on in the green chamber that is you

But I cannot tell you what I most wish to tell you, for there are no words for what I would say.

Could there, then, be music again? Could I sing to you, sing you? Could I take your face as my music lesson and sing?

May it be so. May you be music, for I will never find the words of you, for there are no such words.

How little they seem to me, the words that I have!

Love. Heart. You.

In my head they are rich and reckless, but as I speak them, each becomes a pale cast of what it was.

It could be that I should let words go.

as in a nō play
when a hand rises to speak
and will say nothing

But how should I do that when I know that you keep still so that I may speak? So I go on with these thoughts, which are all thoughts of you, for I have no thoughts but of you and no memory but of you—of you and for you.

All falls.

Other things have gone away.

I have tumbled head over heels down a mountain without end.

This love is harsh. It will draw me away from all that I was. It will, and not with a light hand, take me out from my home. It blasted the me they all know.

But then, it will make me over again, this love. It will show me what I was meant to be, which is us.

all before I bore gifts
keen I held them out in my hand
as one and another went by

now you have given me yours
and in your arm I see mine

We are at a table. We will be at this table to the end of all.

You play your king. I have lost. I love to have lost to you. Now your hand comes over the table.

You say: 'Give me your hand'.

13

Last night I made up my mind: I must go. Now indeed I have done what I could. Now I truly have done *all* I could.

And what was that? End something. Go over all there was up to now, restore it all to my mind one last time, and so end it. I *had* to do that, so it seemed. I had to come to an end before I could find the path to take on from here. I had to look again at what they had given me, all of it. I had to take it in my hand and shatter it, shatter the mould. I have come to see that my path up to now was a path made for me—and it could go on. I do not like it, and I will not take it. More and more I know where it goes.

I have to make another way. I have to find another way. And now I have the powers to do that. I could not do it without help. Help is here: the help I have, now that there is another with me—with me and in me, one that may see with my eyes and give with my hand. I know that what was me will have to come to an end, an end that I will have made. Not death! By no means. But this: I will have left that 'me' and gone.

Up to now my father and my brother have given me the reason I stayed, but the grace that I have seen come over my brother of late—that grace of love, which with him will come to be more—lets me think he could keep an eye on my father as well as I would. It was good, these last months, to see them find one another again a little. Now they may go on from here, and may do so all the better for my being away.

As for him, the young lord, there's no more I may do. I have been sucked in over-long, and I may have done him no good by that. Now he, as well, may find himself. Now he may take his play another way. I wish him well.

No doubt it will be more hard for me to let go of my brother and, most of all, my father—but not as hard as it would be to go on here, as a 'me' I now know to be false. It was not false before: it was right, and true, and good. But that's over. And I'll go without some fare-well speech. When I go from this home—a home that again now is no home to me, no more than the memory of a home—it will not be with a tear in my eye and a piteous look but with joy. And how could I have my father think the joy is at being gone from him?

The command I obey is love's, but it is, as well, mine. Love will be patient, but not for long. Love will look for tomorrow, but wish it here now. I will make my tomorrow now; I will go, in time that love's bended to my will—in love that time's bended to my will, in will that love's bended to my time.

But how should I tell my father, then? By letters? No. And I cannot tell my brother and ask him to speak for me, for that would be worse than nothing. So I have held my tongue with the two of them and come now to see another two— two that by their own love will, I hope, see the reason I have to go: the king and his lady. If I may say what I have to say to them, then they will know what to say to my father. Let my father see nothing of what I will be. I would wish him left with the memory of what I was—left to remember and to know I was what I was *for* him, and for that to be, in his mind, all of me.

I have come to their home, and have with me the things I wish to take: some remembrances of my father, a speech of his in his own hand, a glass that was one of my brother's gifts to me, some clothes.

I know that I will not see my father and brother again. For me to do so, they would have to go as well: each of them would have to look for another path, and I do not believe they will. I wish they would. But I cannot make them, for then the path would not be their path.

When I went from them, they did not look up from the letters they had before them on the table—things to which they had to give some perusal. I went down, my things in one hand. My father could do nothing but redeliver my 'Good morning' to me; my brother's thoughts must all have been with what was in his hand. Then they went on, each to himself more than to the other, lost in thoughts:

'I may not now remember what I call....'

'I would like to think we could have *A Little Night Music* again some time....'

I could go with a light heart. And I did.

One last time I went up the mountain—to where I had gone so long before with my brother time upon time, but now to think—and from there I have come here, to the king's. The watchman at the door, a pale young soldier in state green, was one I know, and he let me in before I had time to ask. I went from chamber to chamber to look for them, touching door upon door (for the lay-out I know), knocking for fear I would come upon them without their expectation of it—for fear, as well, I would come upon the young lord, which I had no wish to do—and at last I did find them. No other was with them. It's been the young lord's way, these last months, to keep to himself.

As I went in, before they could quite see me, I took a look at them. There they are. They face each other quite still, as if lost in doubt of one another. What *are* you? Where have we come from, we two? What have we done? But it could be that all this comes from my own thoughts, as I look at them. Then, as they see me, the doubt falls from each face and the king rises. He does seem quite better now.

'How good it is to see you! Come here to us and be *with* us! Good, good! Would you like something?'

At this he turned to his lady: 'My sweet, what do we have that would not speak woe of the king's table? Is there still some of what we had?'

She: 'The does' eyes?'

He: 'Indeed, the does' eyes.'

'Thank you, my lord, but no', I say. 'I had something at home. That's quite all right, my lord. Truly.'

'As you wish', from the king. 'So.'

It would seem he cannot think what to say, so it's over to the lady, and she goes right to what's on my mind—almost.

'Have you come here to speak of your father?'

I think what to say for a little time, and she goes on: 'It's so good to see him look so well now—is it not, my sweet? And no fear as to his....'

'Memory' (the king).

'Indeed, my sweet', the lady goes on again. 'And how is your good....' She cannot see where to lay down that glass.

'My brother, madam?' I say. 'He is well, madam.'

That would seem to draw an end to these little remembrances, and there is nothing more we have to say to one another. They cannot think what my reason could have been to come here. I, by now, wish I had never done so. But I see that I *must* do what I have come to do, and so I speak again.

'I have come to you on this cold morning to tell you that by the end of the day, when the sun goes down, I will have gone from here. Please do not speak of this to my father, and do not speak of it to my brother—not before I will be well away. I must ask that you do not let them know that I have gone—and gone for good, as it will be—before there could be no hope they would find me.'

The king, with one hand on his beard: 'Gone for good, you say?'

The lady, with one hand shaking in the other: 'Where, but where, my sweet love? And not with your father's wish? O no! No, no! Please, you have to obey! Do as you have been made to do! It is indeed cold out there. You must be here with us to the end! I had it in my heart that you would be the one to—'

But she is held by a look from the king and cannot go on. At that look she becomes cast down, and the effect on me is to make me think I must do something. I take the lady's arm and we go to the window. As we go, I say this: 'Madam, you must know what it's like for me here. Draw the lesson from your own words: obey, do as you have been made. Is that all there is to it? Do you not think—will it never have seemed to you— that we could find other words for what we are? What *reason* to obey? What *reason* to be patient and do what another will ask? What *reason* do you yourself have not to go?'

Whilst I speak she's turned to look at the king again, but we are at the window now, and I have my hand held out, and she cannot but look where I wish.

'Look at the powers before us,' I say, 'on the ground before us. Look down at them, on this morning of sun and turf and hope.'

'I do, I do.' And indeed the lady's eyes look keen.

'Look at them', I go on. 'What may we see? There is a holy father waving his hand. Over there a youth in a green shirt. And that little one by him that may be his brother, touching his brow as he rises now from the grass and lets go of the flowers he had held. A mountain soldier with a beard, and his daughter. Some men over there on their own: they seem lost. A scholar with a long face. They have all come. They do not know what for, but they have come: give them that. Their eyes are raised in expectation. They have stayed up all night for us, some of them. They look at us. They do not speak, for they have no words. Their *eyes* ask. What will this be? What will this be now?'

But, as we look, two do indeed speak—two we cannot see. Their words come to us, and I see the lady look up as well. They come as if from a long way away, and they are grave and profound, the words of watchmen. 'What goes there?' 'Nay,' the other answers, 'show yourself.'

They make me wish to go right away, these words. They seem like words come to receive me in to something I do not wish for. They seem like the words of vows I do not wish to make, and I let go of the lady's hand. But she, with eyes on what I show, cannot give mind to this.

'I see, I see!' She's turned to me. 'There's a bore out there with a look of your father!'

I shatter the glass.

They are gone now—they that had been no more than a form on the glass, made of light. Cold comes in.

'See, lady! There's nothing there! Nothing and no-one! Out there snow falls!'

'No.... No....' She cannot look; she is shaking that not so noble head.

And then in no time at all she's with the king again, and they do something that was not at all in *my* expectation of how this morning would go: They sing. Indeed, they do—as if we could have music again, as if there was no reason not to. They sing as one, the king waving a one-two with his right arm.

There's nothing I would not do
To have you with us here,
But it must be up to you:
These words are not to fear!
Alas, alas, death will come to us all,
But look: you'll have remembrance in the grave!

'You cannot play with me', I say. 'For me that's all over. What comes now I do not know.'

Then, out of no where, I go up to the lady and say this:

There was a time when I held you to be
One I could some day tell my in-most heart,
But now I know that day will never come:
The light is on but there's no-one at home.

But I do not wish to speak thus. It's as if she will draw me in, and I have to come away again to the window and close my eyes so that I may go on with what I *wish* to say: 'But this I *do* know: that what comes will be mine and will be true.'

The king lets go of his lady and comes up to me.

'What is true?'

Before I could say something, he's turned to his lady: 'My sweet, would you let us have some words, O and I, one on one? Thank you.'

The lady goes, and his eyes are on me again when the words of the two watchmen come another time. 'What goes there?' 'Nay, show yourself.' I look hard at the king. He's given nothing away, but I know, as truly as I may see him, that the two watchmen did speak again. Their words make me fear the more. This is the time to go. This is the time when I *must* go. Another night here and the time will be over.

'Do you not like it here?'

'This was my home, my lord, as you know. That's all there is to say. For each of us there comes a day when home, where we have been raised, becomes something *to* which and *in* which we are locked. For many that will be all well and good. But not for me. I find I now have in my hand a key.'

'I think I know him.'

'The key, my lord, is not a he and not a she— which is not to say that love may not be a help.'

'You cannot love and still be here with us?'

His hand is on my wrist. His speech is like a sigh.

'You cannot love—no, my little fair one—you cannot love that youth of my lady's—that lady the two of us have had, my brother and me, one before the other—if not the two at one time. Ha! Think of that!'

His hand now comes up my arm as he goes on.

'If I did, before all this, take some joy in this lady, that day is done—and that night long, long done. I took the lady for reason of state. Are you with me?'

'My lord,' I say, 'all I have come here for is to tell you I must go. You cannot say me nay. What I would ask is for you to speak with my father. Tell him I go on my own, and of my own will. Tell him my mind is made up, as never before. Tell him I know what I face. Tell him I love him, and could never have left if I did not have to. I know how he'll be, but some words from you would be a help.'

'I would have you wish for more—and not for your father but for yourself. Then I would give you more and more and more.'

His hand is on my shoulder, his breath on my face.

'I think, my lord, that I had better go right away.'

Now he's turned from me, and there's a difference in his speech, which comes at me like an oath—harsh, blown.

'You speak of nothing but yourself, to no-one but yourself. You'll never find the one you look for: he's no more than a play of thoughts in your mind. But we cannot tell you this, for some reason. You *will* not take it from us.

'You think you may come here and tell me of *love*'— God, let me not remember the face he made at this! — 'Take a good look at yourself. See if what you think is love is not something you could have better right here.

'You are a poor little lost soul', he goes on. 'You will go out from here and you will find nothing, nothing, nothing, for there is nothing out there for you to find. We are all there is. There is no other "way" you may look for. There is no heaven out there made for you.'

'Be it heaven, be it hell', I say, 'I *will* find it.'

I know I have to keep my eyes on his; I cannot look away.

'Go then. There'll be no remembrance of you here. It will be as if you had never been. The effect of O.'

But now I have turned to go.

I say no more. I have left that chamber of horrors. All I have to do now is find the way by which I had come in, but one does not have to look long for a door—not if a door is what one would wish for more than all other things.

Look: the door is here, where my hand is.
Look: my hand is on the door.
And look: I have gone out.

14

I go out now. I let go of the door, and do not look to see my hand as I take it away.

Snow falls. So: I will go on in the snow. I have my hope with me, and a staff in my hand.

I look up, as if I could see the snow as it falls, as if I could keep my eye on a little of it and see it come down, all the way to the ground.

I cannot. The snow flowers are all like each other, and I cannot keep my eyes on one. I have given up and gone on.

All like each other as well are my treads over the snow, for here, some way on, I have stayed and turned to look at them. In each of them there is now more snow—more in the treads some way away than in these here that I was in before I turned. The snow comes to white them over— white me over. It will take away each mark I made, will take away the memory of my path, so that, when I have gone right away, there will be nothing to see of me and my path. Before long all memory of me will be gone. *I* will be gone.

Now I have turned to face again where I must go.

There is light on the snow still. And there is light *in* the snow. All is still. There is nothing to call to me, no mark to show me the way. There is no-one to speak—no-one but me, and I do not speak. There is nothing. All is white.

I look again the other way, to see the mountain I must have come over. But I cannot see a mountain. All I see is snow, nothing but snow—snow and my treads, which will go in the snow.

Before me—for now I have turned again to look where I must go on—there is more snow. Snow falls over all that was here before, over all that was in my mind. I will have to find how to think again, believe again, know again. The little that is left to me is me: with that I will go on.

It is not as cold as it seemed when I was with the king and his lady. But memory is pale. It means little. It means nothing.

Will is more: my will to be here, in the majesty of the morning, where all is turned to white, where all goes to white—all but me.

Snow. Now. No. O.

This is me, the one that goes on in the snow, which she will mark as she treads, for a little time, and then be gone. What is other becomes white and without feature. She goes on.

I go on in this white: white to make me know what white is. I go on. It is not that I must but that I will. I will go on.

But I could will it another way.

Now I must make up my mind. I take one last look at where I have come from. They will all be there still: my father, my brother, him, the king, his lady. I could go over my treads again before the snow falls quite over them: they still mark the way.

Him. Could I still do something for him that would make a difference? Could I take him by the hand so that, when it comes, I held him from what must be?

The more I have come away, the better I see what I have left, and it becomes like another's memory. Here in the snow I see there was nothing I could do. I was one of his play things.

But it does not have to be like that. Now—with what I know now, and the powers I have—I could make a difference. I could go again to him, and the words would come to me. It could all be turned. And no-one but me could do it. Is that not, then, what I should do?

Now I look the other way, to the unbraced white. I could go on to more of that white.

I could go again over my treads to where I have come from. This time I could make things better for him. I know I could. It does not have to go as they say.

I could do that: go home and not go on.

I could go on, and find what I still do not know.

This way, that way.

I have stayed here to think, and then:

I choose.

let me go on

Well, I did go.

I was out there in the snow.

I have to say it was beauteous, if harsh.

But the cold I did not mind.

It did me good, that cold on my face. Made me keen to go on. Away.

So I went on, never turned to look again where I had come from. What good would that have done? I had made up my mind.

I did not know it at the time, but when I went out the door, and let it close, I had left. There was no other way now. This was it.

So it's all over now, over and done with. Thank God.

It's all over for *me*, that is. They'll go on with it, no doubt. They'll have to. It's all they know, poor souls. They'll find a way. It'll not be hard for them, I know. They'll be all right.

And now I almost wish I could see what they'll do without me.

But no more of that. I have to find what I must do now. It will not be think of them all the time, as I did before.

I have gone from them. Now I have to let *them* go from *me* as well, out of my mind. Let them go, one by one, out the door.

You, my brother, my sweet little brother as was, and then what you are now, one that may not show his love, but I see it, in your face, and you know that I see it, and you fear that some other may see it as well, and this fear will make you wretched. Fare well. Be good to yourself.

And you two: the king that took over from his brother, and the lady he took with him. Did no-one but me see it—how in all you say you speak your shame? Go your way, down and down and down. Fare well.

Then you, my young lord. I do not know what to say to you. I never did. But this now: Fare well.

Last of all I come to you, father. You had from me all I could give you. Then there was more I could not. You did know that, I think. You did know that some things you could not ask. And you did not ask. And, at the time, I could not thank you—thank you for what you did not say. Tell me I have not lost the right to say to you: Fare well.

All of you: fare well. Take my love with you. I would not know what to do with it if it stayed here with me.

Go on with your show. It will take each one of you, in time, to your death. But you know that. You all do. And still you let it, time and time again. Out of the grave you come; each one of you rises, and you do it all over again, as if this time there may be a difference, as if you did not know there never could be, as if you did not know this in your heart, each one of you, but could not speak your heart to one another, but had to go on with it, again, and again, and again.

That wheel: I left it. I went. Look for me where you will; look as hard as you like; I have gone. I have come right away, and there's no way you'll find me—not there, where you are, where you have stayed all this time, never mind what cold charity you receive, time upon time.

Do you hope for mercy one day, for an end to it all, as I did now and then? Well, I sigh for you.

It'll never come. Not there. You would have to have left yourself. There's the fear: to have left yourself. To have gone from what you think you are.

I wish I could tell you all to come away, come away from what you know is death.

There's another way to go on. I know there is. And I'll find it.

But from here I cannot speak to you, and you cannot speak to me now I have gone.

Look: I have gone. No more me. So what'll you do now?

It may be you'll go on as if I never was, make a path over my grave, so that in time all memory of me will be gone, and no-one will remember the one you all did with as you would please.

I never had a say. It was as if all I had to do was see what becomes of me, let it go on, let it take me with it.

But that's the way for you as well, you know; you may go on as if you are the king, the one all must obey, but that's not so. There's something *you* have to obey. It could be you know that. But you have to keep it to yourself.

It never went like this before, did it? One of us goes—one of *you*, I should say.

You'll look for me all over, no doubt, whilst

still you go on with it, your eyes this way and that as you speak your words. You'll wish you could truly tell each other what's on your mind. But you cannot.

But look: here we go again. I say I have left you, but here you all still are, in my mind.

Be gone with you, and take your words with you. 'Alack and alas!' I ask you.

'Belike, betime, bewept' Go on: out! Out!

That was all another mountain and another time.

Let's have no more remembrances.

Now out you go, all of you! You as well, my brother. I did love you, but you have to go. So do you, you two in a hell all your own. And you, my young lord that could not be mine. And you, father. It's hard for me to say this, to you most of all, but out!

I see the light over there.

So again I say, one last time: Fare well!

A

On then.

On then where?

On in to this white, this all-over white, this white on white—this white so white it will have you loosed from yourself before long.

What was you becomes nothing but this white.

White waving in white.

Did I see some light? I think I still do. But now I cannot tell which way my eyes are turned. To see out? To see in?

And what is this 'I'?

You have come on and on in this white, and then the time comes when you—you yourself— are this white, and 'you' means nothing now.

You are non-you.

You are white in the white. On and on you go, in the white, which is not snow now, which is not cold. There's no touching it. But the reason for that is there's no you to do the touching. In your mind there may be something that was you, but look! You are no more.

Hey, but your words go on, as if you still had some being.

So they do. They come with no mind to speak them. They come as if on their own, for the mind's gone that would speak them.

There's no-one here.

Poor O, she's gone.

There's no-one here but us, and we are nothing. We are white, white, white.

We are white words on white, and we cannot be seen.

It would all have come to an end some time, and may be this is it. The end. The white end.

White O becomes a white sigh and then nothing.

And we words, we come to an end.

'Come with me!'

What was that? Is there another out here in this white?

Where did these other words come from? They seemed to come from all over.

Should I call out?

Did I say 'I'?

So this 'I' rises again, at words from another.

But what is 'I' now?

There's the fear it means nothing, the fear of being nothing.

'Come with me!'

'Do I know you, you out there? I did think I was all on my own.'

I speak. There is an I here again.

'Come with me!'

'Come where? Should I do as you say? Tell me, what are you and where have you come from? Have you come to take me where I was before? If so, there's no way I'll come with you. It's been hard, what I have had to do this morning!'

'Come with me!'

'Not again! Is that all you have to say? "Come with me!" When you tell me nothing of where I should go and what I'll find there—not to speak of what you are?'

'Come with me! Come here, and then you will see!'

'See what?'

'Come and look at me here as I sing in the sun, all on my own, all on my own if you will not come and see me, if you will not come and be with me, here in the sun, if you will not sing in the sun with me, so come with me and be with me and sing with me, and you will not be on your own, from now on you will be with me, and I will be with you, your sweet breath, and you will be merry here, I will make you merry here, so please, please, come with me, come here with me, you know you cannot see the sun, so come here and see it, come here and be in it, with me, and the day will not end, no, the day will not end!'

'Now's not the time.'

'Come with me!'

'No.'

'Come with me!'

'Still no.'

'What could make you so unkind?'

'Think you'll shame me by being piteous? I have had it up to here with that.'

'Go then.'

'I will. On my way right now.'

'As you like it.'

'What did you say? Say it again! Was it what I think? Say it again!'

B

No answers. No more that call.

Let him be. This is no time to be reckless. I have come away, all well and good, but to what have I come?

Where is this, all still white?

Which way should I go from here, when there's no path to show me?

There's no-one to give me a hand—truly not him over there with his 'Come with me!' Good I could give him the cold shoulder.

No, it's up to me. It's all up to me.

I have to think. The night'll come, and then what'll I do? I have no home here.

Nothing is as it was.

But then, that was my hope. Difference! That was the draw. Another form of being.

I wish you could be with me as I go on from here, but I know that's not how it goes. That's all right. It's better to be on my own, all on my own at last. I'll think of you as I go, and tell you all I may.

I close my eyes, the better to see what's in my mind. That's something I did when I was—

O memory, when will I have done with you!

The white: it's not out there; it's in here, in this wretched mind of mine, where all that's to be seen is nothing.

Come on! I went up the mountain. That took it out of me. Now I must go over and come down.

I look out again at where I have come to, and indeed there's a difference.

I see a mountain, another mountain, and a path that comes down to me, and on that path there's one I have to call a lady, a young lady, a pale young lady in white clothes, as if she's come out of all the white there was.

I close my eyes and then take a look again. No, these eyes of mine have not deceived me. There she is, as she comes my way with a hand raised, shaking, shaking. She must have come to find me. So how did she know I was here? She must have something to say to me. I take a breath. You keep yourself composed.

She's now no more than a little way away from me, and the words come: 'It's you at last!'

I say nothing. I give nothing away. Does she know me? Have I seen this young lady before? If so, the memory's gone. Have I lost my memory? No, not all of it, not quite all. In a way I wish I had.

'You are with *us* now!'

She's stayed where she is, a little way from me, face to face. We could almost be touching each other, if we had such a wish, which I do not, thank you.

All she does now is look at me, quite still. Close as we are, I have not turned away.

But should I do so, right now, before she—?

Before she what? What do I fear?

Oh, I know what I fear: it's that she means me no good. That's how it'll be. As it was before. There'll be more of them. They'll take over. They'll take *me* over.

That difference I had a hope of, will I find it here? And if not, will it all be as it was again, but with another cast?

Will there be more of them—more than the two there have been up to now: the one I could not see, and this one right before me?

On the other hand, could it be that there's no

more than one being here, and it'll take what form it may wish—call out of nothing one time, and then, when that's had no effect, come as this white lady?

Here she is still. I wish I could ask: 'What have you come to say to me? There must be something. Speak!' But then she does. It's as if she's held a breath and now lets it out, in words, one upon another, all at one go.

'It's good you left, you know. Have no doubt of that. And you left in time!'

In time for what?

'That's good as well, you know. You would have been—. What may I say? That was no... That was not the right ground for you. What more? Well, that's it. It was not the right ground. Not for you.'

And this is? But what does she know of me, and where did she find it out?

'There was no true affection for you there, you know.'

Now that's a little steep—

'Believe me.'

I will, when you give me good reason.

'Oh, it's such a joy to have you here with us!'

'Us'? What's with this 'us'?

Time for me to say something.

'"Us", you say', I say. 'What us?'

That's done it. The words come to an end, and she's like she was before, like something made of wax. From fear? She does not speak. Fear of what? Is she held by something she promised?

I go on: 'There was another that was here before you,' I say, 'but I could not see him.'

She's still as she was.

'He made this call, again and again, for me to go with him. He would sing in the sun: that was what he importuned me with. Sing in the sun. I did not go with him, as you see. I stayed where I was, which is where I have been, all the time I have been here.'

I look this young lady in the eyes. Is it that she cannot take all this in? No, it's more like the light's gone out.

I go on again: 'I fear you'll have to tell me how things go here. Take it that I know nothing, nothing at all, which is, in all honesty, how it is with me. So could you give me a hand? What should I do now? Where should I go? And where have you come from, and what's this "us" you speak of?'

'"Us"?' It's as if she does not know what this means.

'You did say that. Us. You and another. Two of

you. More, it could be. You tell me.'

'Oh that. Well, it would have been the Master
—'

'The Master?'

'No, no.... We must.... I must take you to see,
show you.... Not that, no. What should I say? Give
me more time! Let me have more time here!'

And with that she was gone.

C

'What may I do for your honour?'

I had my eyes still on where the young lady had been, and so did not see him come up the path the other way.

I turned to look at him—and almost turned away again.

What is he? Where could such wretched things as he have come from?

Well, up to now I have seen not a soul but the white lady, so it may be that all the men here are like this.

(Good God, I hope not!)

Each feature is, you could say, out of tune. His left eye is turned up, his right down.

That's not all. His left arm is over-long, so his left hand is close to his knees, waving down there as if he does not know what to do with it. His right hand is held out to me. I do not take it.

His eyes are puffed, as well. Could be he was in an argument with another being like himself.

It must be months he's had that flaxen shirt on, it's so fouled. Is he so poor he could not have donned another? And he's lost a sandal. That bare ankle is a call to my heart.

But I cannot go on like this: look at him, and look at him, and do nothing. I have to say something. That's how I was raised. It's good form, they would say. And what's that? A mould they make for you.

Still, he's a sweet soul by the look of him. I cannot let him down.

'Thank you', I say, 'but I think *I* should be the one to help *you*.'

At this he lets out a moan, a long moan. Does he not know what I meant? And then it's almost as if he would weep.

'Please, please!' I say. 'I wish you would not take on so!'

And there's another long moan, and a tear falls from each of his poor eyes, and all he will say, as well as he may, is: 'Pray! Pray! Pray!', over and over.

'Pray', I say. 'Indeed. I will pray for you. I will pray for you right now. O God, have mercy on thy—'

But with this he's shaking some bells in one hand and waving his other arm in time.

'God have merry! God have merry!' It's like he would sing.

Still, this is better than see him weep, poor soul, and so I sing with him. What reason not to? No-one here to see us.

When we have done, we are a little out of breath.

With his face loosed up now, it does not repel me quite the way it did before. Give him a hat and he would look like a lord. Well, may be not. He's still no primrose.

I sigh, and so does he. His eyes are on me. Mine on him.

'You are a beauty', and he lets out another long sigh.

'And so are you', I say.

'No! No! Not me! But you...'

'Beauty is in the eye of the—'

His right arm rises to ask me not to go on.

'Beauty is one of the true things', he answers. 'Beauty is the light that heaven will show us now and then. We have to be patient for it. But then we will know when we have seen it. And we will remember it when it's gone. Oh, we will remember! "My beauty", I would like to say.'

And now that raised arm comes my way. My hand is shaking, and he must see it.

'No, no: we do not own beauty. They that have beauty do not own their beauty. It is for us, for all of us. It is a grace that comes from God by way of them that have beauty, as you do. The more the beauty will master that beauty, go on as if it's not there, the more the grace, for us all. Is it not so? You must know that.'

What should I say to all this? From him? 'Thank you' does not seem right at all. But then I see that one of his words's given me another way to go.

'"Master", you say. Is there something you could tell me of this Master?' I ask.

In no time at all he's in a state again.

'I have no master! There is no master! There never was a master! There never will be a master! Master, master, master! They have all gone, you know. See: this is all mine again. I may make my own tune. And it does have a tune, you know. More than one. But oh, if he could have let his daughter not go!'

Daughter? Did I at one time know this daughter? The memory's blown. But words come without my will:

'Nor have I seen more that I may call men than you.'

'Me!'

'No, no! That's not what I meant to say! It was this Master—'

'He's gone. To his death for all I know. Did I not say?'

'You did. But before you I had it from a young lady, right here, that there's a Master.'

I see him take a long breath to restore himself to himself before he answers: 'There is not.'

I look at him. There's truly a grace in his eyes. Nothing false could come from this one. But still, he may not know all that she seemed to.

'Where should we go?' I ask him. 'Are you on your way home? Could I come with you?'

'Home?'

'If I could ask.'

'As if such a one as me would have a home! Me a home!'

It's true I do not know how things are here. Does a being have a home, with a bed for the night, and a table, and a light on that table that will be seen from out the window, to show that this is indeed a home? Is it not like this at all? Do they come and go out of nothing, as it seemed that white lady did? All this I'll have to find out, if for me, as well, there's to be a home here—if that's how it'll come out.

If that's not how things are here, then I'll have to have a lesson in how to come and go as I please, to be and to not be.

'Beauty.'

I look at his poor face again, which means I have to look down a little.

'Beauty. May I call you that?

'You do not have to ask', I say.

'Beauty, will you be all right here?'

He must have seen something in my eyes.

'I will', I say.

'Then I'll let you make your way on your own. Remember: if you would like to speak to me again, I'll be there right away.'

'But how will I call you to come?' I say. 'And *what* do I call you?'

But I speak now to no-one.

D

That's left me on my own again. Time to think.

I have something to go on from the two I have seen. There's a Master—must be, given how they went on. The more they denied it, the more it had to be so. From their fear—I could see it in their eyes—may be I should keep well away.

And what's made me think I have to look for some Master? (Master of what, may I ask?) Did I come here for that?

If you look at it, I did not *come* here at all. I *left*. There's a difference. I left, with no thoughts as to where I would end up. It turned out to be here. And I still do not know where 'here' is. All I mind is that it's not 'there'.

I was done in by what I had to be, there. Here, I could let all that go. I could find—what shall I say?—another me. Another me that had been there all the time, in my heart, in my mind, in my soul. Now, with all of *them* out the way, I could draw out this other me.

I did think I could do it on my own, but it may be I cannot. I may have to have help. Whilst I was with these two, all I could think was: Will they help me? But my heart went out—how could it not?—to him, the one you would think had been made up with an arm here, a head there.

As it turned out, there was nothing they could do for me. Well, a little: I now know there's a Master, and may be I should not give up on him (if it's a him). May be I should look in to this more.

Two down, then, and no doubt more to come. Could be many more.

These two have been all well and good, but I have to keep my eye out for worse. Will they come to me? Could be I should go find them.

I have stayed here all this time; now I must go. There's this path that goes up the mountain one way and down the other. I'll go up.

So I do. It's not so hard. Here and there I come upon a loosed stone that's tumbled in the way, and right here it's a little steep. But the sun's up; it's a bonny day; I make my way, and it's all mine.

Each of the treads I take—each one—powers my heart.

But you cannot go on and on like this, O, without let-up! You'll wear yourself out! Give yourself a little time here. Take a breath. That helps.

I look up. It's still a long way. Let's have a little time more. One. Two. Right: on with it.

A tune comes in to my head as I go—cannot think from where. So sing. Whiles away the time.

> *O something mine, where are you something?*
> *You should have stayed:*
>
> > *your true-love's something,*
> *That may sing la-oh, la-oh.*
> *Mind not fashion, o my sweet one,*
> *Showers end, and then are over,*
> *Each young daughter, she will know.*
>
> *What is love? 'tis not here something,*
> *Merry time will make us something,*
> *What's to come is still unkind.*
> *Make your way to find the rich things—*
> *Then come give me what you something:*
> *Youth's the time—oh, never mind!*

Where did this come from? Cannot remember. Well, never mind indeed. It's been a help. Almost there. Not all the way up. But up to this shoulder. Which I'll go over and then down again. See what's there. No expectation. What will come will come. On. On. One, two. One, two. A little more. A little more again and—

Here we are! 'O'er the brow of the mountain!'—where does that come from? See quite a way from up here! Heavens! Make out a hamlet down there. Will not take long.

No, you do not have to go on again right away. Be patient. Give yourself time. You could lay yourself down on the grass here.

I could, but I have no wish to go on being blown so.

Still, let's not go right away. It's such a joy to be up here. Look! See where you have come from. All that way. You did all that.

And by yourself. No-one to give you a hand.

That's right. No-one.

Now's the time to go. The sun's still up—does not seem to have gone from where it was when I was down there—but it'll have to be night some time, and I have no wish to be out in the night, not here.

Down I go, then. Down, down, down.

Should I sing something again? Nothing comes to mind. Do not have to. No-one to make me.

And that hamlet's quite close now. I think I see some... lady, is it? She's come out that door. Which she'll close. She does. And she goes to that table, to sit in the sun, whilst there's still sun.

Soon be there. Then I'll see what she'll have to tell me.

I could call out from here.

I will: 'Lady! O lady!'

'Good day to you! We do not have so many come here. Will you not come in so that we may speak, you and I? I do hope you will.'

So I do, and sit at the table with this lady, and before I speak I look at all the flowers.

For quite some time we say nothing. We are with each other. Words would be in the way.

Then I see she's turned to look at me, and some words come:

'Are you all right?'

'Quite all right, thank you', I say. Then I see I have to say more. 'Your flowers. Quite something. And that herb bed. Rosemary, fennel, rue... —sweet rue's so hard. It never comes up for me.'

'Well, thank you. Truly.'

But lady, as I speak I see your mind's on other things. It's up to me.

'Violets at the door, and a rose that rises from them, like... I do not know what. And an owl-eye daisy in with these columbines. And, oh, a primrose, when you would think it was a little late for them.'

Nothing does she say to this.

'Are these pansies?'

It is as if she does not see me.

'Paconcies, then?'

Still nothing.

'I have to say, it's all quite unmatched in what I have seen.'

Then, to what purport I do not know, she comes out with: 'Are you a Christian?'

A Christian. Something rises in my mind. A Christian. What should I say? Would we all have been Christians down there? Is that it? Did we have pastors with us on Sundays?

A memory comes to me: a hand tenders me something white, and I sucked it up. And another: two speak over me—I lay down and there I was, quite still—and they speak over me.

But come away from all that! Look at this lady you have with you! Keep yourself in the here and now!

'What did you ask?' As I say this I look over. The lady's mind's gone on to other things.

'I say, a little late for a primrose.'

'What?' She's turned to look at me again. Then: 'Oh, indeed.'

More time goes by. Will she speak again?

She does: '"Light" did you say?'

'"Late", madam. For a primrose. A little late. One's expectation is that the primrose flowers when it's still quite cold. Not when it's like it is now.'

'Oh.'

It's as if there's something she would like to say, like to tell me, but cannot. I'll have to keep up my end.

'But it's all so—', I say, ' what shall I say?—so beauteous.'

'Thank you.' Then: 'You seem to know what to call them.'

'The flowers?'

'I never know.'

Time goes on.

'You do well to keep them in such good state', I say.

'Not me. Not me. It's not me.' Head shaking now. Face jangled. Did I say something I should not have?

'I meant no—'

'It's not me!'

'No, no, I see that now', I say.

'It's him!' As if I would know what 'him' she means.

'Him?'

'The master!'

'I see, I see.' *That* him again.

He had gone from my mind, and now here he is.

'I would like to see this Master', I say.

'He's in there,'

'And he's the one that does the flowers for you?' I ask.

'And other things.'

'He's the Master, the lord over all of you here, and this is his home?'

'Well, I call him the master, but by no means is he the "lord" such as you say. He's my other heart, my other soul. He's my O.'

What do you know!

'"O" do you call him?'

'Not all the time. Now and then. Most of all when I sing.' As she does now: 'My love, my O! My night, my day, my O!'

Then she is lost in thoughts again.

'I would still like to see him', I say. 'This master of yours. If for no more than to say how well he does with the flowers.'

'Oh, you cannot. Not now. If you could come some other time? He went in to lay his head down.' She's turned away from me again. 'We have had quite a day.'

What is this? I cannot ask. But then she goes on: 'I love him. You have to believe me: I love him. With all of my being I love him. There's no doubt in my mind, no other thoughts in my heart. I love him, I love him. He is all things to me. There is no grace but he is it. No reason but he is it. No heaven but he is it. There is no tomorrow but he is it. Are you with me?'

I lay my hand on one that's still more white.

'But then I have to go on from there. There is no shroud of mine but he is it. There is no death but he is it.

'I know you are; you are with me in all that I say. I see that. I see it in your eyes. You have been as I have been. You know what I know—which is that love is fear. I do not say that *in* love there is fear—fear that the love will go away, that we will be wretched here in this heaven we have made. No. I say that love *is* fear, that to love is to fear. I look at these words in my mind: "There is no death but he is it." I know that this is true. But I do not know what it means. It would seem to come to me from a long way away but to be here, right here,'—hand on heart, a heavenly look—'as well.'

We each take a breath. And another.

'So it is for me', I say—and some how I must say this: 'Your heart is my heart. You speak from my soul.'

Then right away she rises—and that hand: she's held it out to me.

'You will come again?'

'I will. I have promised and I will.'

And now we are shaking like two watchmen in the night.

It's time for me to be on my way.

E

'Still!'

It's as if I have turned away from that lady, and have gone in to another day—another night, I should say—where nothing is as it was. No lady. No table. No flowers. Now it's a soldier I have before me, one of some bulk that's come out of never and nothing. He's a light in his hand, and he's waving it right in my eyes. It's hard to see. At his command I have stayed where I was, but this is not the 'where' from before. His sword is in his hand and raised. To keep my head I must think what answers I should give him. I must speak truly, but not be reckless, say nothing that would make him think twice. Let's have it all as his expectancy would have it.

'Over there!'

Over there I go.

'What's your reason for being here?'

'I departed this morning from where I had been, and took the path over the mountain to this lady's home—'

'I did not ask you how you come to be here! It's what you have come here to *do* I have to know! We are on the look-out for such as you, such as come here with no right to do so, come at night and do not like the way we do things! But we *do* like it! We love it here! We will never countenance it being other than it is! Take your hand down! Do you believe in the Other Face?'

Well now, two answers here. Which should I choose? It would seem to me that the Other Face must be these they think come here to make a difference. Better if I denied them right away.

'No!" I say. 'May they all go to hell!'

My head's still on my shoulders, so this must have been what he had the hope I would say.

He's so close, and still his light is in my eyes.

'Have I seen you before?'

'You must have', I say. Make out he'll know me, I think. 'Here all the time, me. You know, there's things I have to do here. Keep at it, I do. Up and down. In and out.'

'That's the way! I *have* seen you before then.

You should not be out at this time of night, you know.'

'I know,' I say. 'I was lost, but now I think I'll find my way. Now that I have seen you. I'll find my way all right.'

I make to do so, but there's something more he'll have before he's done with me.

'Before you go, could I ask you something?'

'Ask away', I say.

'Would you tell me one of your... what do you call them? Me and my memory! The things you tell me when you come here. I cannot think of what you call them. You know! It's like music to me, the way you do them. Come on, let's have another one! "Right and Left": that was one. There was this soldier—like me!—and it was all in the night time, and he had let his—Well, never mind now. "And so to bed": that was another one. So let's have another, as you are here. It would be a shame to let you go and not have one.'

I see what he means. He must take me for some other poor soul he's seen here.

'Right', I say. 'Have we done "The Green Dove"?'

'No.'

'Then "The Green Dove".'

I'll make it up as I go.

'One day, over and away, there was a green dove. Now, as you know, most of the time a dove will be white—'

'They will, a dove will.'

'—but you do see a green dove now and again —not here, but indeed there are such things. Look and you will find.'

'A green dove?'

'A green dove', I say.

'This dove,' I go on, 'this green dove of which I speak, had a home with a young lady. Let's say she was Rosemary May.'

'I like that.. I had a go with a little madam that was something May. She had a—'

'Good. The one to find this green dove was Rosemary May's father. We do not know where; we do not know when. He may have gone out in the hope he would find a green dove, but that's as may be.'

'*May* be!'

'Ha, ha!' Better show you are with him all the way.

'He did find one,' I go on, 'Rosemary May's father did, and took it home, to be with him and his daughter. At some time—and again, we do not know when—he died, and left all that he had to his daughter, this Rosemary May: their home, the green dove, and so on.'

'As was right and good.'

'As was right and good.

'Now, the difference with this green dove, more than that of being green, was that it had the powers of speech, and that it had to speak with honesty. It could not say but what was true—what it would know without a doubt was true. It could never speak false.'

'I like that, I do. There's some of your words that go over my head, but I like that. A dove that will speak. And a green dove at that.'

'Thank you.

'To go on, at the end of each day, when Rosemary May will have done all she had to do, this and that, she'll take the green dove up on one hand and go up to bed, where she'll lay it down right by where she'll be, close as you like, face to face. She'll then sing to the green dove, and the green dove'll sing as well: 'Night and day, you are the one....' And there they'll be, all night long. In the morning she'll take the green dove down again, to where she'll have it by a window, which she'll never close, so that it could look out at the sun and the steep mountain and at what went by, and so on, and it would call out from time to time, in the way a dove will. You know.'

'I do.'

'You may think that a green dove, left at a window, would be gone before long, out and away, to find some other green dove. But this one had no such wish. It stayed where it was, by the window. It could look out. It could call out. There was nothing more for it to wish for. It had all it had to have, there with Rosemary May. It had all the joy it could hope to find. So it stayed where it was, and let the young lady go on with what she would. Sewing, it could be. Shaking out the bed clothes. This we do not have to know.'

'No, we do not have to know.'

'But one day—and I should say here that Rosemary May did not keep the doors locked—one day she comes to the window where the green dove should be and it's not there. She's something to give it, and it's not there. It's gone.'

'Oh no!'

Good. He's still with me.

'Right. "Oh no!" is what she well could say when she comes to find the green dove gone. As well as: "Shame on you! Shame on you that stole my green dove!" By now she had one arm raised and was knocking hard at the door by the window. 'Shame on you!' she went on. 'You took away the joy of all my heart and have left it cold, cold as death!"'

'"Cold as death." That's good. Death is cold. I have had words with death now and then, I have.'

'All hell was loosed.

'Now, it could well have been—and you could well think—that the green dove had gone by himself, if it was a him, and let's say it was, that he had left and gone away. But no. There was indeed one that stole him, and took him away, but then let him go. Out there, away from home, the green dove did not know what to do. So it did what it would do at home, which was nothing. From where it was, it could look up and down. It could call out, if it had the wish. It could do all this, and it did. Now that it was out, it stayed out.

'Out there, as night comes on, what goes on in the green dove's mind? Well, which of us could tell what goes on in the mind of a green dove, if we believe that a green dove could have a mind?'

'That's true! Do I know what goes on in my own mind all the time? I do not! There was a time we had to find out what they had done with some—this was in.... Now where was it...? Oh, this head of mine.... But go on. Please!'

'Night and day Rosemary May went all over to look for it.

'No-one had seen it; no-one could tell Rosemary May what to do, where to look.'

'No-one....'

'No-one.'

'No-one in all this....'

'No-one.'

'And there they all are!' He's shaking his head. 'I see them now! If you could but say to them: "Think! Is there nothing in your head? Think!" That's what I have to tell my men all the time.

'Oh, but now I know what it was, that time when—. But go on again, please! I like this one—but not, I have to say, like I did the last one I had from you, which was, you know.... Well, do I have to tell you? But go on, go on. Never mind me.'

'But they did not.'

'What did not?'

'These that Rosemary May went to ask—ask if they had seen the green dove, but not one of them had.'

'Oh right.'

'Then at last Rosemary May did think, and remember that if she would go out and call the green dove, no more than that, it would speak, and she would find it.'

'It would speak! The green dove could speak! Think of that! In words! Speak in words!'

'It could. So she went out again, and made this

call: "O my green dove, o my green dove, speak to me, come to me!"

'But the dove did not think it was Rosemary May's.'

'Did it have a reason?'

'I do not know if the green dove had a reason. It may have done. It may not. It does not say.'

'What does not say? The green dove?'

'No! What I keep knocking my head to tell you!'

'All right, all right! Keep your shirt on!'

I truly should—and keep a little away from him.

'They had a home', I go on, 'with each other, but that was all.'

'They ....'

'Rosemary May and the green dove.'

'Right. I see. Go on.'

'And so to this it would say nothing.'

'I lost you there. To what would it say nothing?'

'Rosemary May's call.'

'Right.... So?'

'Remember the words: "O my green dove, o my green dove, speak to me, come to me!"'

'Still not quite—'

'*My* green dove, *my* green dove, when the green

dove did not think it *was* Rosemary May's green dove. The green dove does not see things that way.'

'It does not?'

'It does not. So may we please go on?'

'All right. Some hope I'll make this one out....'

'No, you are all right. *We* are all right, you and me. Hey, two watchmen in the night.'

'Go on, then.'

'This is close to the end now.'

'Cannot say I mind. You know, you have been better at this. Last time, like. That was a good one! O my, o my, that was a good one! That had my little lordship up to look for a hand!'

'Well, that's good to know. Now you see, Rosemary May was so close to the green dove—close in their thoughts, they had come to be, she and the green dove she had been with all this time—that she did not take long to see she had not done this the right way—'

'Come again?'

'It's that she would know how the green dove would think. From being with him so long. That's all.'

'If he had a mind and thoughts.'

'Indeed.'

'Which we do not know.'

'Let's say he did.'

'All right. Go on, if you will.'

'And so she went out again, to call again, but this time she did so with other words: "Where is the green dove? Where is the green dove? Speak to me, come to me!"'

'I see.... Think I do.'

'But a green dove's thoughts do not go with one's expectation, and you could almost see this one think: "I may not be the green dove she means. There may be some other green dove, that I do not know of. There may be two; there may be more than that. What then? I should say nothing." And so it was.'

'Does it go on for long like this?'

'Not long now.'

'I'll not say: "Good."'

'Then Rosemary May went out one more time —and this would be the last time, believe me—to call with still other words: "Is there a green dove here? Is there a green dove? If so, say so! If so, speak!"'

'"If so, speak!" I love it!'

'The green dove took a little time to think: "I thank Rosemary May for all she does for me, but she does not own me. And she cannot call me '*the* green dove' when there could be some other. But a green dove is a green dove: that cannot be denied."

'Mind made up, the green dove now answers:

"'Here! Here is a green dove!" comes the call from the steep mountain. "Not yours, and not one with no other like it, but truly, without a doubt, a green dove!"

'And it left the mountain to come home, and went in at the window again, and stayed to the end of time.'

'It dove down!' Do you see? The dove dove down!'

'Indeed. The dove dove down. End of.'

'Now before I let you go, *I* would like to tell *you* one.'

'Right you are.'

'There was... let's call him a soldier. He's in love. A soldier in love. And there's two he's in love with. A he and a she. And these two are in love with each other.'

'I see. I do see.'

'*See*: that's it! They do not see his love. They are so in tune with each other that for them there's no other music. He may sing; they will give him no mind. He may sing his heart out and not have to fear the shame of it. When he's with them—one of them, the two of them—he'll do all they ask. When they have gone again, up with love, he will weep.'

'And he cannot give himself away.'

'He cannot.'

'My heart's with him.'

'The one is his master.'

'"Master" did you say?'

'His master, indeed.'

'And the Master of you all? Do you know this Master?'

'Let's say I have done.' I see him look away. 'His master. He must give his all to his master's love, give his all to his master *in* love. Nothing may be left out. He must do all he could. And the other, his master's love (and his), he must honour with his soul.'

'It is quite a state to be in, a piteous state. So it turned out how?'

'It's not over.'

With that he was gone.

F

It's still night, and now I have to have this:
  'Here we are!'
  'All of us!'
  'Some on their way!'
  'How many?'
  'One I know well is not here but will come.'
  'So which of us is that, then?'
  'You'll see when she's here.'
  'Oh, that one.'
  'And there's another that'll be here before long.'
  'So that'll make two more of us.'
  'Could be more than that on the way.'
  'But more of us are here than not!'
  They come to me.
  'We do indeed.'
  'We are here.'
  'Again.'

In my head.

'That's us!'

'Us again!'

'What should keep us away—'

'—when we see we could help you?'

'You know we'll not let you down.'

Out of the night.

'What did she say?'

'Night.'

'That we come out of the night.'

'Does she know we are here?'

'Out of the day as well, some of the time.'

And out of the day.

'She does.'

They come to me.

'Let's see what she'll do now, what she'll say!'

They say what they will.

'There she goes!'

'Ha! All of you! May we keep it down a little?'

They ask what they will. Of me. They are all in my head. I know that. They are not truly there. They are, you could say, made of words, nothing but words. Words without a face.

'So you may think...'

'You know that's not how it is.'

It's been like this all the time I have been here. It rains words in my mind, and they go on and on, and I have no way to keep them from this. Was it like this before?

'Before what?'

They come to me, and they ask me things to which I have no answers.

'Like: "What is time?"'

'But we would like to know these things.'

'And there's no-one but you we may ask.'

'No-one.'

'It's us and you.'

'Us and you, lady.'

'All the time.'

'Which of us was that?'

'Was it me?'

'You should say: "Was it I?"'

All I may do is not speak to them.

'I should not!'

'You should!'

'Not!'

All I may do is let them go on for as long as they will and say nothing to them.

'We'll draw you out!'

'That we will!'

'Come on! Hadst tongue in't th'head?'

They think they'll draw me out, I know, but if I go on with what I have to do, which right now is go on down the mountain to see if I may find some help, some steward to take me in, and if, here and there, I play in some words they do not know—'

'Oh, but we do!'

'We know all your words.'

'They are what we have to make do with, as well as you.'

'You know that.'

'If you would look in to your mind—'

'—look in to your mind—'

'—you would see each one of us is you—'

'—on each of us there's your face.'

'Hey, you should say it the other way!'

'Right. She's the one with the face that truly comes from us.'

If I could find one to take me in for the night, all would be well.

'So you may believe.'

Then in the morning—

'This is not the right way for you to go on.'

'We see it's not the right way.'

In the morning—

'Not the right way at all.'

'Not at all the right way.'

'There's no "steward" for you to find.'

'You know that.'

'That's right: you know that in your heart.'

'You'll be out in the cold all night.'
In the morning—
'That's the reason we are here.'
In the morning—
'To help you on your way.'
'To counsel you.'
'To keep you from being lost.'
I give up!
'That's right: give up!'
'We know what you should do!'
'It's your good we have at heart!'
'So give up and speak to us!'
'Ask us what you should do!'
Never!
'There you are! You *did* speak to us!'
It would seem I must. What are you here for?
Again.
'What you'll give us!'
'What you'll tell us!'
'You know we have to have one of these things.'
'One of these things you tell us.'
'You make them up—'
'—and you tell them to us.'
I should say that when I speak to them—
'What?'
'We are here!'
'It's us you should speak to.'

'All the time.'

'We are not "them", madam.'

– I do not speak out. I form the words in my mind. As well as I may.

'We'll help you.'

Thank you, but no.

'Come on, you have been here—'

'—all this time—'

'—and what do you have to show for it?'

'What?'

'Out there they'll tell you nothing.'

'But we will.'

'You should give more mind to us.'

'That's what we are here for.'

'That and nothing but that.'

'To help you, remember?'

'We'll help you remember what you have to say in each speech.'

'"Each speech!" That's good!'

Speech?

'In your play.'

'The play you are in right now.'

'As we speak.'

'Ha! Another good one!'

This lady is not in a play.

'But you have been.'

No, I have not.

'And you are now'

'We all are.'

No!

'It's all right.'

'Have no fear.'

'We'll not speak of *your* play—'

'—the one you have come out of—'

'—and the one you are in right now.'

'There's more to choose from.'

'*Love Letters Lost*: remember that one?'

'What was she in that?'

'*King Rich Two*.'

'Oh, I remember.'

'Tell me then.'

'*The Merry*—what was it?'

I fear you know more of this than I do.

'It's true we do: *As You Like It*.'

Oh....

'"Oh" indeed.'

His words, from out there, when he had given up on me.

'Still doubt us?'

When I had not gone to him to—what was it?

'Sing in the sun.'

Thank you.—No, I'll be dupped if I thank you!

'Still think we are not up on what's what here?'

'And the lady in white. Know what she was?'

'And then him with his left hand touching his knees?'

O my God...

'Thank God it was his knees.'

'The one in love—'

'—I think we may say—'

'—with his unkind master's daughter.'

'And the soldier—'

'—another one in love—'

'—one in love with two.'

'And now—'

'Us.'

'Us.'

'Us.'

'So what play have you come from?'

'Which one?'

'Tell us: which one?'

'We know, but we have to have you say it.'

'She's in no mind to give answers.'

'What's she up to?'

'Let it go.'

'No, she should know how things are here—'

'—how this is where you come to—'

'—when you have left where you should be—'

'—when you think it's time now—'

'—time to "find yourself"—'

'—the "true you".'

'What's that then, when it's at home?"
'Ha ha!'
Please go now.
'We cannot go.'
'You know that.'
'Not before you have done as we ask.'
'Not before you tell us what you must.'
'We have stayed out of the way before.'
'And we may do that again.'
'We will.'
Please do.
'But there are things you should remember.'
'Must remember.'
'Like: You are the one that may speak—'
'—but we are there as well—'
'—of you and in you—'
'—but may not speak—'
'—not speak as you do—'
'—speak out as you do.'
You make me out of breath.
'And there are other things you should know.'
'Like: where you have come to.'
'Like: what you'll find here.'
'One that was a true saint.'
'A king that lay himself down.'
'A youth that had been a scholar.'
'Remember him?'

Tell me no more.

'We have to.'

'Some come here and never go away again.'

'We must.'

'But there are some that go in to another play.'

'If not the one they had been in before.'

No...

Is there no way out?

'That we cannot say.'

'We would if we could.'

'You know we would.'

'We are with you, remember.'

'All for one and one for all.'

Do you not see what you have done to me?

'Do not weep, lady.'

'If you do, weep well.'

Do you not see?

'We do not see, lady.'

'We cannot see.'

'We wish you well.'

Will you all please go away!

'We cannot do that right away.'

'That's the way it is.'

'You have to tell us one of your things—'

'—one of your things for us to take away with us.'

'You know this.'

'You made one up for that soldier.'

'Now make one up for us.'

'Then we'll go.'

You have promised?

'We have.'

'We all did.'

I give you what you ask and then you'll go?

'We will.'

All of you?

'All of us.'

And not come again?

And not come again!

'Go on with it!'

'Then we'll go.'

'You know that.'

All right, then. Here we go. Let's call this one 'The Bended Window'

'Good! One we have not had before!'

That's right. And we'll call it 'The Bended Window' as there's a window in it and this window is, well, bended—bended at one end.

'Good one!'

But you'll have to keep still there.

'We will.'

'You'll have no more from us.'

'Not a breath.'

'Nothing at all.'

Right. So let's give it a go. 'The Bended Window'.

There was a king, and he was locked in his home. And the reason for that was that another king took over and had him locked up so that he would be out of the way. But this other king, the one that took over, had mercy on the king he took over from.

Let's say the king that took over was 'B' and the one he took over from, the king from before, was 'A'. That'll help us keep an eye on which is which.

'Good call!'

'Keep it down!'

Now, King B took mercy on King A and had given him a sweet little home to be locked up in all the time. It had all he could wish for: a bed chamber for him and another for his lady love, a closet with clothes for the two of them, staff to look in on them. All King A had to do was keep himself there. His lady love, as well. They could not go out. Never.

But in this, again, King B had mercy on them. Never mind which way they would look, in that sweet little home, there was a window there. So they could look out and see, as it could be, the baker's over the way. But that's something we do not have to go in to.

Now we come to the key feature: the bended window, the window bended at one end. And there's more to it than that, for there's another difference with this window, which is that when you look out of it what you see will be way out of all expectation. Window upon window will show, say, sun on the grass, but out the bended window it rains. Out of window upon window you would see day-light, but the bended window would look out on night.

'How could this be?'

'Come on, tell us!'

'How come this night in the day time?'

You may well ask. As for King A, he *did* ask . On his staff he had a scholar to give answers to such things. Let the king's scholar come. Let him look at the bended window and look out of it. Let him speak.

'It could well be', let this scholar say, 'that what you see out this window is, my lord, how things have been at some time before. It may, in the morning, show us last night, my lord. It may, my lord, show us a night many months before, which we do not now remember. It may show us when it rained long, long before we could have been here to see it, my lord. This, my lord, is a window to what was.'

King A faced his scholar: 'I like how my scholar answers. This is how it must be.' And he turned to another courtier: 'Give him some honour. What honour does he not have?' 'The Green Hand, my lord.' 'Scholar! On your knees!' And the scholar did so. Then King A raised him up: 'You are now a Brother of the Green Hand. Do not shame this noble honour!' 'I will not, my lord.'

So that was that.

And so it went on. Night in the day time. Day in the night. Snow when no other window would show it. A hat blown over the grass.

Then one morning some young cock took a look out of the bended window and what did he see? He could not believe it. Had his eyes deceived him? He took another look. No, they had not. There it was.

He went to call the scholar, and now the two of them could see it. No doubt at all.

Should they tell King A right away, before he was up?

'Before all that, you should tell us!'

'So you should. What was it?'

What do you think?

'We cannot think!'

'You are the one that should know!'

'So come on: tell us!'

Out on the grass, where it could be seen from the sweet little home King B had given King A, out there, quite close by, was a grave.'

'A grave?'

A grave. With a grave-stone. And a lady, turned away from them, with one pale arm over this grave-stone.

The scholar went away to look this up. There had never been a grave there, over the way, where this one now was. No-one lay in the ground there. Not a soul.

What to do?

The scholar could not make out what was on the grave-stone, but he had a glass with which to see things some way away, and he held this glass to his eye.

Now he could see what was on the grave-stone. The bended window was not, it turned out, a window to what was. It went quite the other way.

'May I take a look?'—thus the young cock that was with him.

'No'—and with that the scholar cast his glass

to the ground, to shatter it, and there it lay, its powers gone. No-one now could see from there what was on the grave-stone.

'Will you tell us what it was?'

Be patient.

Before long King A was up, and the scholar went to tell him there was something to be seen out of the bended window that had not been there before.

'What is it?'

'A grave, my lord. With a grave-stone, my lord.'

'And there is something on this grave-stone?'

'It cannot be made out, my lord. Not from here, my lord.'

'Well, you know—do you not?—that I cannot go out from here. That goes for my lady love, as well. So you must go out and see what is on this grave-stone, and come here again and tell us. Do it now, my scholar, Brother of the Green Hand. My heart is all tumbled up and down by this.'

'But, my lord, the bended window cannot but show things that are not there. If I go out, my lord, I'll see nothing.'

'Still, do as I command!'

'I will, my lord.'

So the scholar went out, and, as was his expectancy, could find nothing. No grave. No grave-stone.

When he was in the sweet little home again, he went to King A.

'There is nothing there, my lord.'

'Come, my scholar! Come, my lady love!'

And they all went to look out the bended window, where they could see a grave, and a grave-stone, and a lady, turned away from them, with one pale arm over this grave-stone.

'There is something on the grave-stone, is there not?' (King A).

'There is, my lord' (the scholar).

'Then what?' (King A).

'I cannot make it out' (the scholar).

'No more may I, with my poor eyes' (King A). 'Which of my staff would have good keen eyes to see what is on this grave-stone?'

'There is one, my lord' (the scholar). 'I will go and find him, my lord.'

So there they are now: King A, his lady love, his scholar and the young cock, all at the bended window to look out.

King A: Do you see what's on the grave-stone?

Young Cock: The lady's pale arm is in the way.

King A: But still, do you see something?

Young Cock: Letters. One here, two there.

King A: What letters?

Young Cock: T and O.

King A: Right. 'To.'

Young Cock: Then I. Then it could be S, it could be B. Then A, some way down. Then DILD, I think. That's all.

King A: This means nothing. Do you have a glass, my scholar?

Scholar: No, my lord.

King A: I think you do!

Scholar: No, my lord. It had such powers, my lord, but lost them.

King A (he would know nothing of such things): It died, so to speak.

Lady Love (with some fear at these words): Let it be, my love, let it be. These things are not for us to think upon.

From that day on, all the bended window would show was the grave, and the grave-stone, and the lady with one pale arm over the grave-stone.

'Would we could see that!'

'Is that the end?'

That is the end.

G

All this time I stayed where I had been when I was with the soldier. But with my mind on *them*, I did not see the sun come up and go down again, all in no time at all. (I wish it would not do this.) Now I have come to, and here we are, out on the mountain again. The lady of the flowers should be right here, by the path, but she's gone and so have the flowers—herb bed and all. And it's night.

No-one's here, so let me think some more.

Could it be true? Was it a play? Was it a play that I left? And is this another?

In a play your words are given you. You do not make them up yourself. You have no say. That's how it is.

We had a play like that—more than one. And now I truly must remember how it was down there in 'Denmark'. It cannot all be let go—not now that I know what I know. To know where we are, truly to know, will give us the powers to go on—to make things better.

Does it seem right, then, that I was in a play, and all I could say was what some other lay down for me? That was the wheel, and all of us turned it?

A state without hope.

But look, if the words are all given you, what they say is not. If there's love in them, you have that love in your heart, with all its expectation and its hope, all its light of heaven on the morning grass in a day that goes on and on whilst the sun's stayed where it is and made the night go away as if that night was nothing more than something seen, let's say, out of a bended window. I know these things. It's become *your* love. It's not that it would seem that way: it *is*. And these are *your* words.

What becomes of you, then, if you left the wheel? If you went away, as I did? Have you lost your words? Not at all. You come here, if you believe them. This is where you all come.

If that's so, the lady of the flowers and the lady all in white—and the soldier, and that one with such woe in his countenance—would all have been in a play of their own.

Could that be the way of it?

If that's true, does it help me? If it's not true, does that?

Does it help me find a way on from here? Does it help me find a way out? Does it help me find that other me?

How could you tell if you are in a play and if you are not?

I cannot go by what *they* had to say. *They* could have had their words all given them. If not that, they say they are with me, and most of the time they do seem to be, but they have a will of their own. Each one of them.

I have to take in what they say but not believe it all. I have to look for more of these down-at-heels that made their way here. Most of all, I have to keep my mind on what I have come here for.

I have done what was hard: I left my father and my brother. That's all over. But it's left me without something. A soul? Is that what I meant? Not quite. More a soul to be at home in.

'There will be a day—'

O my God! This is not one of them again, is it?

'—to tell it thus: it is all almost done.'

No, that's not in my head. It's from over there.

'This is not that day.'

'What are you, that come in the night out of

nothing? I cannot see you. Have you been here some time? I know you are not in my head with all that chorus, but where are you? And what are you? A being like me? Tell me!'

No answers come.

'You speak of a day to tell me it's all over, all almost over. Tell me now: is it close, that day? Will I be there before long?'

Still no answers.

'Are your words not meant for me?'

Nothing.

'What should I call you? You seem to be one, but are there more of you?'

'I speak. It is I that will speak to you.'

'You speak as one, then.'

'That is so.'

'Your words come as if from out of time. Where have you come from?'

'I come out of the night of death, a night that will have no morning.'

'You come, but you have not gone—you have not left that night?'

'That is so.'

'I was right that you are not in my mind?'

'No, not to find me there. Not to find me at all.'

'Is there more you have to tell me?'

'What is it you look for?'

'Thank you. Good of you to ask. Not so many do. But I do not know quite what to say. Do you have something I could call you by?'

'I do.'

What?

'All they will let me tell you is that I was a king.'

'Then I should call you "my lord". What time is it with you, my lord?'

'Two.'

Two in the morning?

'Two at night.'

'How was it you died, my lord? It may not be mine to ask this, so please say if you cannot tell me.'

'By my brother's hand.'

There is a fear comes over me. 'Thank you.'

'Please, do not weep! No, do not weep! Help him, some of you!' For I in some way know, but cannot see, that now there are many of them.

'Let us do all the good lady could hope for.'

'Thank you.'

Is it all in my head, how two of them have held him, each with an arm?

'I cannot see you, but I know you took him with you. Thank you. Lay him down so that he may find his breath again. And then you may all go, you and he, to where you have been all this time—to what and to where you have never left, if you are as he is, and I know that you are.'

Now it's almost as if I could see them on a path as they take him away, and almost as if I could make out what they say as they go.

'It is no joy to have died for a king. Pray for us. Be of good heart.'

That had some grace to it. Should I thank them before they have quite gone?

Thank them for what? What lesson could I take from them? This one that was here—the 'king'—was he here indeed? Was he not, alas, again something in my mind?

No. He was a memory, a memory I had almost lost and had no wish to remember.

You call up the dead—no, you do not call them up: they call on you—and they have nothing to say to you. Nothing that means something. Nothing you could take in. Nothing that could help you.

H

'Look up!'

Where have I come to now? Which way did I go? What it is to be lost....

It's day-time now, but there's nothing I remember from before. No mountain. A coach went by over there, which was right out of my expectation.

'Look up here!'

Well and truly lost.

'Please! You should look up here!'

Is this another call from over yonder, like I had from him out there in the all-over white?

'No!'

Help! Does this one know my thoughts?

'I do, I do! But please, look up here and you'll find me!'

Up where? Up the mountain? There's no mountain.

'No! Up here! Over where you are!'

At which I have turned my head to look up and it's true: there she is, way over my head—not that here it's not all way over my head....

'O my sweet, do not say that!'

'I did not say it, if you remember. It was not meant for you. Do you have to see all that goes on in my mind?'

'Now please, I have come here to help you!'

'Thank you, but what help could you give me from way up there? Come down and speak to me!'

'I cannot do that.'

It's not in your powers?

'You may say that if you wish, and I'll not take it to heart, but tomorrow you may know better. As it is, I cannot come down to the ground to be there with you; that's not how it goes.'

'Does this have something to do with the Master?'

'My father?'

'Not your father, no. Well, it could be your father. May be. What does he do?'

'Did.'

'My heart goes out to you.'

'Please, say no more; this is a good day. He made honey. What a perfume it had! Look where you like, you cannot find honey like it now. Up to the day of his death he made it. He made it with love; that's what made it the more sweet. I have so little I cannot give it away, but if I find more, I'll give you some.'

'Thank you. Lady, I wish I had more length in my arm, so that I could have it raised up there to be with you! Think of it as being there now, on your shoulder. I know what it is to have lost a father.'

'Please, let it be. I have come here to tell you where you should go.'

'To find the Master?'

'No. That's not for me to say. All he'll let me do—'

'He?'

'Please. All he'll let me do is show you where to go to find another, another to tell you more than I may. I do not know what she'll say, but I know she'll give you more help.'

'How do I find this lady?'

'Go over there and then down, and you'll come to the Well of the Sun. You'll know when you are there.'

'How?'

'It'll speak to you.'

'What will speak to me?'

'The well. Words will come out of it.'

'The well! What words?'

'That I cannot tell you; it will not speak to me.'

'Something like: "Well of the Sun here. Thank you for your call. How may I help you at this time?"'

'May be so. As I say, this is all more than I know. And now I must wish you well and go.'

'No! When I have come to the Well of the Sun, what then? How do I find the way on from there?'

'The well will tell you.'

'I must ask a well?'

'It will tell you. It will not be false with you, not with you.'

'I ask it where I should go?'

'Ask it what you like. It will give you all the answers you could wish for.'

'And you will not?'

'I cannot.'

'Well, it must be you could tell me this: What play do you come from?'

'I have to go now. It's a joy to be here with you, but I cannot take you all the way like this. He'll not let me.'

'He again. But what play?"

'A joy, as I say. I have another little tune in my heart now. But I cannot go on with you. You must know the affection I have for you—have had for you for a long time.'

'Let me ask you again: What play?"

'Now look down at the ground!'

Did she see something I would have tumbled over? No, there's nothing there—not a stone, nothing.

I look up again to where she is.

That is to say, I look up again to where she *was*.

Will you believe me if I tell you that I did go on and come to the Well of the Sun and have the Well of the Sun speak to me?

No, you'll not. And you *should* not. That's not how things go here. I cannot tell you what's not true—true as I see it, that is. If you come here yourself some time, to where this is, and I still do not know where this is, you'll no doubt see things another way. I could believe that. It's all so jangled in my mind, and hard to speak of. There are things I have left out, things I do not know the words for, things that there do not seem to be words for. Things you would not believe.

But never mind all that. I have come here, to

where I think the Well of the Sun must have been, but it's all long gone. There's a stone here, a stone there. That's it.

Did she up there know it would be like this? Have I been had? And by which of them? She up there made it seem she did all she could for me.

But was it all the Master's say-so? This blasted Master! I more and more think he's out to do me down. If not, what's his reason not to show himself? Never mind which way it is, I'll have to lay eyes on him some time.

There's nothing left to do but close my eyes and see if my mind will, with the memory of how it is, see how it was.

As a well, it must have gone down, down, down in to the ground, and if you took a look in to it, you would see the sun down there—see it at never mind what time of day, for the reason that it turned in the ground all day long, little by little, to face the sun. And that's how it could speak. As it turned in the ground, so words would come. Something like words. If you had gone to the Well of the Sun to see what it would say to you —tell you what was to come—you would think you could make out words. If two of you had come, there could well (ha!) have been a difference in the words you made out. To one the Well of the Sun would speak of love; to the other it would speak of death. Something like that.

That's how it could have been. But these are no more than brief thoughts. Brief and light. They do not go down, down, down.

I | J

If the Well of the Sun could still speak, would it have given me some help? Would it have had the powers to show me the right way on from there? I doubt it. These things never do as they should. You are better on your own. You look what's before you and you choose what to do—look at the music but make up your own tune. And sing it.

At the Well of the Sun I take the path to the left. It's a long path, and before the end of it the light goes as day's turned to night. I have to find a bed for the night, I think again, and right there I see a home, up to the right of the path. It's almost as if I made the wish come true. There's a light in the window by the door, which would seem to me to say: 'O you out there in the night! Do not go on when you could have come in and stayed here! Come in, come in! Restore yourself! We may not be rich, but we'll do all that we may for you! For you and yours! There'll be a bed for you here! And it would please us to have you with us at table! If you have something with you that we could all take some of, better still! But we have no expectation of that! So do not go on! Come in!'

Should I go in then? I have been knocking here, and that's not raised them. No more does shaking the bell over the door.

I see if the door will give way at my hand, and it does, so I go in.

There are two of them—two young ladies, that is. And please do not blame me that I seem to find young ladies all over. And do not ask if there's a reason. How should I know?

But let me think. Is it that, when you are here, all you see is yourself, again and again? If not, could it be that they have all come here to have a lesson, say—a lesson in never mind what?

Now my mind goes cold. Is their lesson one in which they have been given words to speak, words they must speak to me, for which they will receive a mark at the end of the day for how well it went? Was that the reason they (and I do not know *what* 'they') let me come here? Is all this made for me—for me and no other but me?

But look, there they are, these two. And there is expectation in their eyes. I should say something. I *must* say something.

'Good day!' (for the sun is up now again, in so little time). 'Thank you!'

Time goes by, and there's nothing from them, so now I have to think what more to say.

'Thank you, that is to say, that you let me come in and be with you, in your home. Not many would. Not so many would have left their door not locked. Not so many at all. Not where I come from. If you ask me where that is, I'll tell you. But I do not like to think of it right now. You know how it is. You have left home, and you have no wish to remember it. Something like that. Something a little like that. It's hard to say—hard for *me* to say, to speak of, to remember. You know?

Still they say nothing; still they look at me.

'I hope this is a good time for you', I say. 'A good time for me to be here, that is. If I may do something to help, please tell me. I would like that: to help. Sewing: I could do that. If you had stockings that could do with sewing, please let me know. Please let me have them. Here, right away. Let me do that for you. I could make you some clothes whilst here—for as long as you would wish me here, that is. It would be such a joy to me, to give you a little help in your home! Please believe that. There are other things I could do as well. Please let me! Please tell me!'

I go on like this for the reason that they do no more than look at me and say nothing. Now I cannot think what more to say, so I look at them. The two of them are like each other, in feature as in stature. There is that look in their eyes: of expectation. But do I make it out to be worse than it is? Their look could be one of patient mercy, as if this rained down from heaven out of their eyes. I do not know. They have me shaking. It's how the face of each of them is still, quite still.

And then when I have given up hope they will speak, they do, the two of them at one go:

'Come in, come in! That's it, come in! Oh, have you done so? My, my! Well, never mind! It's so good to see you! Not so many come by now, you know, and not all of them that come by will take the time to lay a hand to the door and see that

'So here you are, my sweet! How good it is to see you! So good! It's been a good long time we have been here to see if another young lady like we had before would lay a hand on the door and see that we are here, and know that we will do all we

we are here, and know that we will do what we may for them. But please give no mind to what she'll say, this one here on my left. She'll not mind *what* she'll say. Never did. So you should not mind it. If you do what I tell you, you'll be all right. As I say, we do not have many come here now —and what are we here for if not to help? —as if there could be another reason for us to be here, right by the path, as you could see, and for us to have left the door so that a young lady such as you, a young lady that had come by, could find she could come in and be with us, with the two of us, that is, for

may for them. It would please us to do that. That's what we are here for. We are not rich, but we do what we may. But there's something I should say before I go on some more, which is this: that you'll find I'll be the one to show you the way, show you how things are done here. Not this other one, by me. You may well think we are two, but we are not. We are one and one. We are heaven and hell. We are morning and night. We are now and never. That's not so hard to remember, is it? No, I see you are with me. I'll not say more. That may be left for another time, when we have a bed for such a young lady and we have things we could give such a young lady as would come in, which is what we hope, and we have been here like this, have stayed here like this a long time in the hope that you, if not another like you—not that there could be another like you, I know—would come in here and be here and, it may be, would have stayed here some little time, as long as she would wish, but it could be a he, we do not mind, that could be better, in a way, but I do not have to go in to all that right now, we have to know each other a little more we may speak to each other one on one. Another time. Indeed. I hope there'll be such a time, before you have been here so long that—. Well, I have promised you, and you must take me up on it. Before we have that time with one another, you and me, you should keep an eye on me, and you'll see from my face what to do and what not to do, for there are things you should know that I cannot say to you right now, not for as long as she's here, do you see? I know you do. I see it in your eyes, the way you look at me, and have been. I did not have to tell you, did I? You

before we tell you all that we could tell you.'

could see it for yourself. So remember.'

'Please, please!' I say. 'Please do not go on like this! I cannot tell what you say, I cannot make out your words, if the two of you speak at the one time!

'That's the way we do things here, little lady!'

'If you do not like it, you know what to do!'

'Well, may be it's all right for some, but I find it hard. It's as if the two of you are in an argument with each other all the time!'

'Well, it could be that we are! Would you like to give that one some commerce in your little mind, again!'

'You have been here so little time and you like to think you know all there is to know of us two! Think my sweet?'

'Would you please not do this and see if you could speak one at a time? One of you did say, I think, you had gifts. This is all I would wish to be given: that you each speak for yourself and then let the other do that. Givers should not be unkind, you know.'

'You see what she's like?'

'A little know-it-all.'

'Oh well, this is *your* home and so you do things your own way. Let's see if I may keep up with you.'

'That's better. Do not look for the reason things are as they are. Take it as it comes.'

'It's time for you to say something, so tell us, please, where you have come from.'

'That's quite hard to say', I say, to the lady on my right, for these words I could make out. 'You see, we would call it "Denmark", but I do not think it truly was Denmark, not the true Denmark. It was more a Denmark of the mind, if you like. I cannot tell you the reason I think this now, but I do. Away from there, it's come to seem something false, something made up.'

'What's the reason you have this doubt as to where you have come from? Where did you say it was? Oh, indeed. I have not been there for some time, but when I was, I did find I had a good time there. As it is now, I cannot

'Never look for something true in a state! They are all made up. There's no reason for them to be as they are. They are so for the rich, as I see it. All they are is a tune and a memory. That's all. We should have no more of them!

go out the door without I have to have this lady come with me. You see what a state you find me in!'

Down with the state! If we wish to have a state at all, it should be another form of state: a Green state!'

I have lost almost all this. I would like to find out if these two come from some play, which I may do if I tell them more of what I now have to see was mine.

'Could I tell you a little more of how it was there?' I ask.

'If you have to.'

'Please do!'

'Well', I say. 'I had a father—'

'So did I! My father was a king—I speak of a time long gone now. He did not have such good counsel; his memory should have had more honour than it did. But there we are. He did what he could.'

'I think we all did. My father was a lord. I did find him a little harsh from time to time, for on some things we never could see eye to eye, and he *would* have his way. You know what a father's like.'

What to do? Go on is all.
'And I had a brother—'

'So did I! Two of them. They had gone away, and had been away for some time when I was little. How was this...? I cannot think now. I did find them in the end, but that's a long—. No, you go on, please. Your brother.'

'I did not. Did I wish I had one? Cannot say I did. But it could have been a help; indeed it could. Another to play music with. Another to speak for me. Another at my arm. But no, let's have more from you.'

I cannot not remember. I know now that I have to face up to how things went and what I was. If I do not, I cannot go on. But will they?

'There's no more to say', I say. 'I had a brother. I would like to know something of yours.' I have turned here to the one on my left.

'Thank you. They are good men, noble and young. But I have not seen them in a long time. Let me think how this was... I had to

'You should not ask. This one here'll tell you that she left home to look for two men, and that she did find them in the end, if not some

restore them to father. They had had another father to see to them, but now was the time to have them home again. She'll tell you I had nothing to do with all this, but that's not so, not so at all.'

way before the end, for it goes on and on, the way this one'll tell it, and you'll be dead and in your grave before it all comes to an end. You'll find it all goes on and on to the end of time.'

'Thank you', I say to the one on my left. Then, so that she'll not be left out, I say 'thank you' to the one on my right. Before I may say more, they are at it again.

'Did you love your brother?'

'This is all such a bore....'

'Indeed I did', I say. 'Indeed I do, I should say, for he's still with us.'

I do not say this, but in a way he's not, not still with us. This is not the 'us' it was—if it's an 'us' at all. What I should say is: He's still with them. But do I think he is? Could I not hope he's left as well? Could he have come here by now, to find me?

But when, O, will you say what you have to say, which is how you have come here to find yourself, to find another you, which you hope these two could help you with?

They have stayed still as I went away with my thoughts, and now when I look at them again, it all goes as it did before.

'Tell us of this brother of yours; I would like to know more. Does he, tell me, have a lady love? Would he have left your father by now and be master in his own—?'

'I would give my soul to be away from here. If I could, I would go up and look for some things for this maid to wear, other than what she's come in.'

'Master!' I say. 'That was it! That was what I meant to ask you: What do you know of the Master? How could I find him?'

'There is no master here. There's no-one to tell us what to do. It's not like that. We rose up, you see. So we do not have a king here, not now. And nothing like a king. One day we did. But that's over.

'I'll help you all I may, but you'll have to do most of it yourself. Do you remember the thorny rose to the left of the path that took you on from the Well of the Sun? It's such a joy! Comes out when

There's been no king here for a long time.'

'Rose?' I say.

'Indeed. But that was all long before we had come to make a home here, so I should not say "we" but "they". They rose up, and out with the king it was. So there's no master now.'

the snow's gone. It must be out by now.'

'Indeed. Go to that rose again and say this: "Bare bier bore, Here to for, Tell me how to find, What I have in mind." Then think of what it is. This will make the rose speak.'

'Thank you', I say. 'This is good to know, and could well be a help. You never know.' I do not ask to go right away, as that could form some doubt in the mind of the one on the left. And still there's been almost nothing from them of what and where they have come from, the reason they left.

'Would you tell me,' I say, 'each of you, one at a time if you would, of your most sweet love, of the one you keep in your heart and will not let go, never mind what becomes of him? Would you do that for me?'

This should do it.

'If I have to…. A soldier. My love was a soldier. That means he had to be away from time to time. Did I tell you I was a king's daughter, so there was nothing they would not do for me, most of all when my soldier was away. Still, there was one there that did not wish me well at all. Not at all. I'll tell you the reason another time. But here's how it was. This one comes to me when I have gone to bed.—No, it's not what you think: there was nothing of that. He's come to take something of mine, which he'll take to the soldier and say he's had it from me and more. Do I have to go on

'With all that heart of mine I will! I will with joy! But how to say this? What will you make of my words when you have not seen him? Ask me and I will tell you! But what good is that? You would have to see him, to be with him, to have his breath on your face! He rose up to my window. At night. We had seen each other a little before. Before that, I did not know there could be such things—such a one as he! As I say, he rose up to my window. I see it now: we speak to one another of love; we say we will be wed in the morning. We have promised this and we are. There was never a

with this? He was honorable, my soldier. When two of you are like this, and you have longed for each other, it will have to come out as it should. That's how these things go. You know that as well as I do. So let's say that's all there was to it. My soldier's had to go away. He's made to doubt. He comes home again and, at last, there are things that will restore his mind. We may now be as one. All's well that'll end well.'

doubt in my mind but that he would prove true! He is there when I come, and we are wed. He is my true love; he is my lord, the one I will honour for all time, as he will me. He is my honey; he is my rose. You must keep that in your thoughts: my honey, my rose. And now I cannot remember what we did then. We are wed, and we have a night of love, and.... It was all good. I know that. But I cannot now remember.'

I think I know them. I know I know them now. The one took a long, long path that went here and there, all over. The other they would keep close—that was how it was then—and not let out of doors. The two of them come to the one end: dead with a dead youth by them—but this is not death for the one, and for the other it is.

But where does all this come from, that I did not know I had in my mind?

'Thank you, madam', I say. 'And thank *you*, madam. It was hard for you—for the two of you —to say all these things, to remember all these things, but you did, and I thank you. This meant more to me than I may say. But truly I should go now. Before it becomes night again—and you never know when night will come here, I find, never know how long it'll last. Indeed, it is night almost all the time. A brief day, and then night will come and would seem to last for months, so you would think.'

I look at them one last time, one and then the other. And they look at me, as if they could see in to my soul.

Have I seen you before?   Have I been you before?

My hand is at the door.

K

'Me the king!'

I have come out the door, and it's still night (if not night again), and here's another of them in my face, and he goes up and down, up and down, with his 'Me the king! Me the king!' And then I see over there another one that would seem to think he's sovereign, never mind that he lost his soul on the way.

'Please cast your eyes this way to see the true king. Thank you.'

And that's not all: now there are two more of them that call out from some way up the mountain:

'There's no more than one king here, and that's me!'

'Do not believe these heels! What they say is all false! If you wish to see the king, here he is! Me!'

And then there are still another two that call to me to look their way, and so I have turned to see them, and there they are, and they have some-thing to say as well:

'Now let's have this right, shall we? We must call on Reason to help us here. Reason would have it that there cannot be more than one king at a time. That's how things are. There cannot be two. I believe we all know we are in the one state here, and one state will have to have one king, if it is to have a king at all, which some do not. One king, I say. Not two. And by no means more than two. There may be two in one day, if one king should have died that day, so that another will have to be king that day and go on from there. But still that's not two at one time, and there's no other way there may be two in one day. You could say to me—and some have—that you would like there to be two for a time, to see how that went, but I would have to tell you that this could never be, no how, no way. I hope you are with me. And I know you'll all wish to have your say on this one, but if I may keep on for a little more, this was all to prove that there never will be more than one king, never will be two, let us say, if these two have breath in them. Now, to be brief, how it is here goes thus: there's more than one of us that'll call out all the time that he's the king, which means not that there's more than one king but that there's more than one that *would be* king, if he had his way. Would you please keep this in mind? I hope you will.'

'Do we have to have all this? Look this way and you'll have to say: "He is by right the king!"'

And now that I have turned again, I see there's another I had not seen before.

'Please, please, all of you! You, over there, you call on "right", as you call it. But come on, right will tell you in no time at all that the king must be a soldier—'

'That's me, a soldier!'

'You think such a one as you becomes a soldier? No, I was the soldier of all of us here!'

'You never could see what I had in me! You never would believe in me! A soldier I turned out to be: a soldier king!'

'I was a holy king.'

'I thank God I was not there to see it!'

'I would pray night and morning.'

'God help us!'

'And *I* was a soldier!'

'You could never be a soldier!'

'You died young!'

'It's not so hard, you know, to make out here

which of us is king and which not. I have the majesty of a king, which means that I must be the king. That's all there is to it.'

At this I see that two more of them have come, out of nothing.

'Rose upon rose: it is time for the rose!'

Oh, the rose.... I remember. Thank you! I must find that rose.

'And heaven will tell you that the true lord here is—'

'Me! You cannot speak the words, o father mine. Your day is done. What you left I took up. Time will go on.'

The argument, as well, goes on, and I know I'll have to give it my all: 'YOUR MAJESTY!'

They all look my way.

But almost as they do so, they are blown away by other words that come to me, from one I know.

L

'O! O! Is this you?'

That call!

I cannot make out where it comes from, but the youth himself I know....

'My brother!' I call out to the night. 'Where are you? I cannot see you! Where are you? Where are you?'

'Here!' A hand is touching mine, and I take it with my other. There's almost no light, but his face is so close. No beard still. Never will have. May be he would if he stayed here, now he's come. But will he?

'Is this you?' I ask. '"You, you and no-one but you?"' That was something we would sing, at a time long gone. 'How did you find me?'

'I did, like, go all over. But then I think: Where

would she have left *from*? So I go up there, and I see with my little eye....'

'Oh, in the snow? There was still the snow? You could see my treads in the snow?'

'Right I could. So then it was, like, go! go! go! and let's see where that lady's gone to! There they all are—may be out there now, for all I know—one by one by one by one. It's like they ask me to go where you have gone. Like they say: Out of here, brother!'

'You know, I had no such wish at the time, but I see now—'

'"Oh, let me not show my hand!" Is that what it was? Come on, O, you are so out of it!'

'Like you, with your A–Men Two.'

'Do you *have* to remember that? My Sweet Lord!'

'And your Violets.'

'My youth, when I was—never mind. So that's what I do, like. And I made it here.'

'I did not think... Let's say I had no expectation you would do that. But now that you are here, my, it's good to see you!'

'And you!'

'Quoth!' I say.

'Quoth!' And now he's held up his hand for mine.

'But there's more to it than that', I say. 'What have you come *for*? Did *they* ask you?'

'There is, as you say, more to it than that.' And he's turned away from me to say this.

'Then what?'

There's more light, and I see him take a breath.

'Do I have to tell you, O? Come on, do I truly, like, have to tell you?'

Another breath.

'I know what you'll ask. That I should go and be with you all again, and it'll all be as it was? No. I cannot do that. And do you blame me?'

A little time goes by before he'll say: 'No'.

'Then that's all there is to say. You know what they are like. I have come away. And you may not know this, but so have you. How would it be if you stayed, if you stayed here with me?' (I do not at all know if I truly wish him to do this. There are things you have to do for yourself, and a brother could well be in the way.)

He's shaking his head. 'This is not my fairground. It's not where I have to be. And it's not where *you* have to be. You know that. We are made to be *there*, with them, in Denmark.'

'You made it out', I say. 'You have gone over the mountain. That's it. It's all over now, for you. Be here. Find yourself here!'

'No way!'

'Way!'

'O, there are things I have to do at home.'

'You still think of it as home?'

I look in to his eyes. What does he know? Does he still believe all this, that he's in Denmark there, with the King of Denmark, that he's a courtier?

'You have another reason to wish to be there', I say.

Will he show some honesty with me now?

We look at each other, and it's as if, with his eyes, he did say something of a love with such powers over him that he cannot speak. I see a tear.

Then it's over.

'The king—'

'Was he the one to ask you to come?'

'No! How could you think that? Let me tell you, O: I have come here of my own will! Out of love, love for you, you poor little gis! This is not, like, where you should be! Do you know where this is? From what I see, all they do here is remember and remember—all the time. There's a perfume of the dead and lost. But we are young, O! We are young! God, do you see what they call fashion here! This is not where you should be and, you know, still be you.'

'That's it!' I say. 'I have no wish to be me—me

as I was. I have to find another me. It's in here'—I lay my hand on my heart—'and it's up to me to find it. As of now I cannot tell what it is, this other me. It may be something I do not like. It may be something that it'll take me some time to see as right, to know to be right.'

'I love what you are, O.'

How could I doubt this?

'But do I now have to say to you:' he goes on, 'I love what O was?'

My sweet brother!

'I fear for you, O.' He's cast his eyes down and does not speak to me face to face. 'I fear you have, you know, lost your mind a little. Like, here you are: the O I think I know. But—Lord love us!—I do not know you, O. I do not know you at all. It may be I never have done.'

Lord love us. Something father would say. Hard to go on now. But I must.

'Which of us'—I look down—'could say what it is to know another—indeed, what it is to know one's own heart and mind?'

Then his eyes are on me again, and I have to look at him, and his face is harsh. 'I know what I must be. Do you?'

'There's no "must"', I say. 'We all may choose. You may choose.'

'Oh, you think so? How little you know!'

He's up as if to go, but then he's turned again to look at me. 'The king would like to see you again.'

'Him? He may have a reason.'

'And there's this. I wish I did not have to say this to you—'

'Father. Is he not well?'

'He is well; he is well.'

'Go on.'

'You remember how he comes to his death?'

'How could I not?'

'With him now it's like it's a true death, like he'll be dead and gone. Each time it's like that. Each time more so. He goes on with it—you know what he's like—but his heart's not in it now.'

I see in his eyes there's more he'd like to say. 'Go on,' I say, 'if you have more to tell me.'

'I know I should not say this, not to you, O, but it's, you know, like he's given up. Without you there. You should see him.'

'Do not ask that.'

'O, you should see him.'

'Please....'

'You should see him!'

'No.'

I meant to say 'I cannot' as well, but he's left me no time.

M

'My sweet one, o my sweet one!'

But did my brother go? Is he not still here, in this night that goes on as if it would never end?

And where are we now?

'Is that you, my brother?' I call out.

'It could be, could it not?'

But that's not him. And it's not like him to play with me this way.

'What are you? And what have you come for?'

'Ha!'

'Show me where you are!'

'Here. By you.'

'But you know I cannot see you at all.' I say.

'Then what if I do this?'

A rose light comes on, and we are in a bed chamber. A bed. Green bed clothes.

He's raised a hand and there's music:

> *The way I like it*
> *Is the way it is*
> *I have mine, (do it!),*
> *He's had his...*

It's all given me the horrors. To my mind—but what do I know?—it's like this is where a lady of the night would do what she had to do. I have to say I do not like being here at all. And I do not like the look of him.

'How did you do that?' I ask. 'You turned on the light. How the hell did you do that?'

'Ha! There's more I could do if you would let me, young madam. '

'Come close and you'll rue the day!'

'What would you do to me, then, young madam?'

'Do not call me that!'

'What?'

'Young madam.'

'If you say so. As you like—'

Before this goes on some more, I say: 'Look. There's a door over there.'

'Do you have to be like that?'

'Look: I have come here for a little help. Which I do not think I'll have from you.'

'You ask me to go?'

'I do.'

'Then I'll honour the lady and go.' Which he does.

I see the door close and then, in no time at all, there's a knocking at it.

'Let me come in! Please!'

'No.'

No more knocking.

I let some time go by, and then I go to the door. It's locked.

Now it's me knocking.

'Let me out! Let me out!'

'If you'll let me come in again.'

'No.'

'What if I do this?'

I look away from the door. The bed's gone. The green bed clothes have gone. It's all bare.

I cannot speak.

'Like it?'

I do not know what to say.

'If not, there's this one I could do.'

And in no time there's a scholar in here to give a lesson, and they all come in, and go on as if they cannot see me.

Then the scholar's turned to me. 'I like this one. Hope you do.'

It's him.

Whilst it would seem he goes on with his lesson, his words are all for me.

'Tell me: what did you come here for? Then we may go: you your way, me mine.'

With all that's gone on, I truly cannot think. My mind's not my own. Will he now help me? Not be as he was before? What's come over him? Was it something I did? And what did he ask? Oh, right. It'll take me some time to think which of many answers I should give. The things that have gone on here.... My brother. Before him these men that all think they should be king. Before them—Ha! It was one of the two ladies.

'A rose', I say. 'Could you tell me how to find the rose? There's a rose that will speak, so they say, and I have to find it for it to tell me the way I should go.'

'Where did you have that from?'

'Two ladies. They have a home with each other. They speak at the—'

'I know. Which of them?'

'I think it was the one on the right. But it may have been the one on the left. There's quite a difference.'

'There is. And you believe them? That is, you believe the one it was? You know, one of them cannot but speak true; not so the other.'

Mercy me, how should I know which was which?

Whilst my mind is up and down with all this, I say: 'I do not know, my lord, what I should believe'—but as I speak these words cold fear comes over me, and without a breath I say: 'I have nothing other to go on.'

'I like you, so I'll give you what help I may. All is not as it may seem. Keep your eye out. You have seen how you may be—'

'Deceived. I know.'

'Could be that's the reason you had to come here, to take a lesson—from this scholar, right? —in what is true and what's not.'

'How do I know what is true?'

'Look at it in the light. Look at it with your heart. Look at it with your mind. Look at it, if you may, with your soul. One of these will tell you.'

'Look, it's a little late in the day, but could I ask what to call you?'

'Rich. That's what they all call me here. Rich.'

'Well, thank you, Rich. I should be on my way. Could you let us out of here?'

As I speak it's all gone: the door, the table, all of it, and we are out on the grass, and the sun is up.

'Look out for yourself, O.'

He's held me by the wrist, then lets me go.

'You know me?'

'We all do by now.'

'How many more of you are there, Rich?'

'You'll find out. Not so many. Now, you look out for yourself.'

'"Yourself" you say. That's almost what I have come here to find. But it's hard. One day I think I may be on the up; then in the morning I'll be down again. Some of it's being here, where I never seem to know what to do, and where I cannot find my way, and you all—well, most of you—would like to help, but for some reason it's never turned out as it should, you know? Then again, it could be all me.'

'No, it's not you. It's how things are. We have all been there. But then you may choose—'

'Choose what?'

'Nothing. There are things I should not tell you, things you'll have to find out.'

I look at him, and he gives me a perusal that gives nothing away.

'Shall I see you again, Rich?'

And then I think better of it.

And know not to ask again.

Then he speaks: 'Tell me again: What did she say you had to find?'

'A rose.'

'Right. It may not be what you think. And that was not all. You would then know where to find....'

'The Master. It's him I have to see, but for some reason I have to go by way of this rose.'

'That again is how things are here.'

'Thank you, Rich. I know you know more than this but cannot tell me.'

'We are all on the look-out, O. That's what we are here for, all of us: to find what we most wish for. There's no one way. You'll have your way, which will not be my way—which means there's no more than a little help I could give you. Almost no help at all. But one day you'll be there. You may not find him at all. It may be that he'll find you.'

'Thank you for that, Rich', I say.

'But then what will you ask?'

'I'll ask.... I'll ask where and how I'll find another me. Not the me I have been. Another.'

'I see. I see it in your face, O. This is something you have to have.'

'It is.'

'That's how it is for all that come here. There's something we have to have, other than what we have had.'

'What's yours, Rich—if I may ask?'

'Never mind that. On with you.'

I have turned to go, but then I think of something I must ask.

'Rich, which was your play?'

By the time the words are out, there's nothing there.

N

That'll take it out of you, that will! Goodness, what a one he was!

I should tell you: she's gone for a little time. So you'll have to make do with me.

When it's all done, and he's gone, this...what did he call himself?...she comes over to me to say, right in my face: 'I have had it up to here!' As if I was the one to blame!

But I could see she was done in, so I say she should have a lay down, close these green eyes. I'll take over. She give me a look. It's all right, O, I say. (I call the lady 'O'. We all do.) I'll not tell one of my...you know.... No, it'll all be quite lady-like. Have no fear. So away she goes.

As she's not here, I could tell you what I make of all this.

But should I?

What the hell....

You see, it's all this 'other me' to-do. It's not for me, that. I have one me; what would I do with another? Could be they would speak, the one of them to the other. Could be they would not. May be one would have a go at the other. And where would I keep another me? And then there's this: What is a me? Do you see it? No. Will it speak? No! It's me that does that. That's to say, I think it is. Does it have a heart, a head, like I have? You tell me. Will it give you good counsel? Will it be there tomorrow? Will it go away, and you'll be left by yourself? God love us, this'll do my head in!

But here she comes, up from bed. Time for me to go.

○

I have come a long way, to where there's another mountain, and there's a light up there, so harsh I cannot look at it. I think it must be the light of the sun on a glass window, but I'll go up and see.

You may have to be patient here as I make my way up. Most of the time there's nothing to speak of. Oh, a robin over there. Would be good if it would sing. But no. Could be the cold.

There's no path, but if I keep on the stone I'll be all right. If you go on the turf, you find it comes away with your treads.

There's still the sun on that window, if that's what it is. It'll show me the way. Not so many come up here, so it would seem. If more did, they would, over time, make a path. Could well be no-one's been up here in months. Months and months. Does no-one look in on him, the one that's made his home up there?

I should have gone to look for that rose, but there's something that's made me come this way. Some draw. The sun on that glass window. The one that'll come to the door.

Do not know what I'll find. Could be a scholar, up here to take a close look at the sun. Better, he'll think, to do that on his own. Have all his time to himself. For the things he'll have to do. And there could be another scholar (you keep yourself to yourself), up here to look for flowers that have not been seen before.

If not a scholar at all, the one up here could be a watchman, to keep an eye out. There could be two of these observers. More. What do they have to look out for? Men from the Other Face.

I think some more, and in no time I have come all the way. Indeed this is a home, but I have to take a breath before knocking at the door. It would have been better to come up when the sun had gone down a little, but there we are. Here now.

From here I may see all the way over to that other mountain, which could be the one I had to come over from 'Denmark', if that's what we should call it—which I cannot see at all, as it's all the way down. I cannot see it, and it means nothing to me. That's where I was, and I did not know what it was. That's where my father still is, and no doubt by now my brother.

I have turned from it all. There's no window that the sun was on; this fair home, all the way up here, is all made of glass. No-one comes here, so he must not mind if he's seen.

Oh, but the one in there is a young lady, on a bed, but she's up and quite composed. I seem to think I know this young lady from before.... But where? Could she have been the one with the flowers? The one that stayed up over my head as I went? The one in white? It's hard, in my memory, to tell one from another.

So it's not a he up here. How one still falls in to this! But she could still be a scholar. She could still be a soldier. And I may find out before long.

There's the door. Over I go.

At my knocking the young lady rises. She comes to the door. We look at one another, face to face.

What is this? Fear? Ecstasy? Are we head over heels in love with one another in no time at all? Is she blown away like me? I think she is.

I should say right away that there's nothing of dalliance in this. She's no libertine and never will be. I see that.

She's held out a hand to me, but then she took

it away again, as if touching would be more than she could do with.

Which of us will speak? She does.

'Oh my God! You look like me!'

'No', I say, 'you look like me!'

'You could change clothes with me—', at which I take over, '—and no-one would see the difference!'

'You know what I'll say!'

'Most of it!' I say.

'The two of us wear green and white!'

'All the time, me!' I say.

'Me too. But come in! Come in! This is all too... I do not know what! Look: let me hold the door for you!'

And so I go in.

Now that I have done so, it's as if this is *my* home as well, the home I now remember, but did not before—as if the memory, long lost, comes to me again.

Think of it. I cannot tell you what it's like; you have to think of it, think of how it would be if you could see yourself in another's face, if you could look at another hand and think it was yours—if you could look at another hand and *know* it was yours. If two could be one, and never more than one.

We go, hand in hand, to that bed I had seen. 'Lay yourself down, and I will too.' The words seem to come to me from over that other mountain, but she is right here by me.

We are in that state of grace that I wish I could speak of, but I know no words that would do it.

I have no wish to do other than she'll ask. We look at each other.

'What are you? Where have you come from?'

I do not know which of us these words come from.

'Give me your hand again.' 'Take my hands in yours.' 'Do you mind if I lay my hand on your face like this?' 'No, I do not mind at all.' 'May I do that again?' 'You do not have to ask.'

More words, that no-one may say they own.

'What may I call you?' Now I know this is she.

'O', I say. No more than that.

'O! O! O! Is it a sigh? Is it the night-time call of an owl? O! O! O!'

'And you', I say. 'What should I call you?'

'There's never anybody here to call me anything.'

'Then what do you call yourself?' I ask.

'O-fie.'

I cannot quite say it the way she does, with a long 'O' and a long 'I' that goes on and on, but I give it a go: 'O-fie.'

'O-fie and O', I say. 'O and O-fie. Which is it? Let's have no argument!'

'No, no, as you say! Anything but that!'

'Well, then', I say, 'I'll be two if you'll be one.'

'And I'll be one if you'll be two.'

'Then that's done with', I say. 'Tell me all you may of yourself.'

'You'll know it already.'

'All what?'

'Already. Like: by now, from before. Already.'

'I'll remember', I say. 'There are words of yours I do not know.'

'We have been away from each other a long time.'

'Indeed we have. But now we are with one another—'

'—and we'll go on that way for good and all!'

'O-fie!' I say. 'Sweet O-fie!'

'My O! My dear heart!'

It goes on like this for day upon day. Each morning I think: I should have left by now. Each night I find I have not.

And it's hard to tell how long I have been here. A day is like another day. A night is like another night.

'All is still', I say to O-fie. 'There's no "is" and "was" and "will be".'

'It's Mountain Time, O.'

I wish I could go on like this. I know I cannot.

Tell yourself, O! What have you come here for? It was to find another you: remember? O-fie is not that other you. You did say that. You did say so yourself. She's a joy, but this path the two of you are on—the one of you, you could say—is not the right way, not for you. Before long you'll have lost the will to go. She'll see this as well, and she'll think she's to blame. Should she make you go? Should she close the door and keep it locked?

'O-fie, do you think we could have some music?' I ask. 'This morning's one when, if you are like me—and I know you are—, you deject yourself, never mind what you do.'

'Oh, my O! But what did you ask for?'

'Some music.'

'Do I know what that is?'

All right. This is one of the words I know and she does not. There are some where it's the other way.

'Music, O-fie', I say. 'La-la-la, la-la-la. I would like you to sing to me. Will you?'

'The ear's appetite!' And now it's me that's lost.

But sing she does.

It's a green day when I see you,
A white when you are away,
The small light at the window,
The cold of come-what-may.

We stood upon the mountain,
You leave to go on down.
All I have now's remembrance,
And you, you are on your own.

'Is that how it'll be, do you think?'

That could have been O-fie, could have been me.

Other things:

'Are you more yourself now, with me by you?' Again, I cannot tell you which of us this would have been.

'I love you in that green shirt. It's so you.' This was me. That I know.

'You took the very stoniest path up here, you know. You found the way, but here's another I'll show you.' O-fie. Had to be.

'Will you unclasp your hands, my dear? You are secure here. You know that.' O-fie again.

'While I was all alone here, did you *know* that I was?'

'No. Never.'

'If you had, would you have sought me out?'

'How could you ask that!'

'Tell me something. Make it up if you like. It does not have to be true.'

'When I speak, you think this is yourself.'

'That could be true.'

And then there are things we play, like:

'How many words can you make with these letters?'

'What letters?

'These letters.'

'A, B, I, O, S, T.'

'And N, and W, and Y.'

'Saint.'

'Away.'

'Nony.'

'What's that?'

'Look it up.'

'I will.' Then: 'It's one of your words, not mine! I object! Sophister!'

'Shall we take a poll?'

'A poll of two?'

'That do not wish for more', she said.

I cannot tell you the effect of these last words on my soul.

And she'll make up things the way I do:

'Time out of mind, there was a prince. I do not know what he was a prince *of*, but never mind that. There's no reason for us to know. It may be better not to.

'Now, most of the time, in something like this, if there's a prince he'll be noble and fair and earnest and steadfast and attentive to the ladies and do good things. This prince was not like that. He had a beard and was careless....'

Now and then I was not up for it. I had to go. But I had no wish to go. I stayed:

'There was a worthy man of wit and wealth withal, and thence—'

'Another time, O-fie. What it is to be down like this....'

And there are so many other things I remember from how she would say them:

'It is a privilege I have received.'

'Lovers' tokens are not to be lent only but given.'

'Your shoes!' (I call them 'shoon'.)

'What do you mean when you say you are a maiden fearful and pitiful? Are you not ready?'

'We have vowed that if one of us dies the other will not be lagging.'

'Christen me again then!'

'Till mid-morning. At the latest.'
'My flower.'
'I would be bereft.'

'Tell me another one, O-fie.'
'Tell me one of yours.'
'I will do.'
'Promised?
'Promised.'
'Would you take vows on it?'
'I would.'
'Well, then:

'Out there in a time without time, the Green Lady is still alive. At night she will look for an opportunity, and in the morning it could be that your heart will have been stolen. Cold, dead cold you will be, but walking, you could still be walking. You still have a pulse. You are not laid out, and your dear love grieves over you. There will be no alteration in you to show that the Green Lady would have been in bed with you all night and stolen your heart.

'No-one—*no-one* parts with their heart with a good grace. It will have to have been filched from you. You will have to have been distracted by what she did to you. She grips you. Silent, she will have moved in to your bed, and she grips you, and right then she will have stolen your heart, and little by little you will be forgetting it all, for that, too, she will have charge of: your mind, and what it will remember.

'In the morning they may say to you: What is the reason your window is all splintered? Did anybody cast a stone at your window and dashed away? Did *you* do this? And you will not remember anything: not these green hands on you, not how you grow there, not how she stood as she untied these green garters, not how she jests with you before, not how she could teach you there is more to your nature than you could believe, not the cunning in these green eyes, not the quick green showers that would come over you, short but so pleasant, not the gallery in full green light in which you seemed to be fixed firm as she did what she did, not the great green jewel that adorned that green breast, not how she holds you, not how she's touching you as she's gathering your heart from within you to leave you cold and with no remembrance.'

Ungartered she was.

There are some things I do not speak of to O-fie. Most of all, how we all here may have come from some play or other. I still cannot quite believe this, but that's not the reason. I have not raised it as I have no wish for us to speak—to think—of things that have nothing to do with how we are right now.

For me, to be up here is to be away from all my doubt and fear down there on the ground. Here I may love O-fie without shame. And it's so for O-fie as well, I know. We are so close.

But I have stayed here a long time—over-long. This was not what I have come here to do—to find. I have to go.

I do not think it out. I may have left some of my things. But here I go, down the mountain. I have not turned to see if she is there to look out from that glass home. I have not turned, and I will not do so.

P

I have not come all the way down what I will now think of as O-fie's Mountain when it's as if all the bells of hell call out. There, a long way out, the 'Lady Grace' is being blown this way and that, tumbled up and down. Men draw on something I cannot quite see, and as they do so they sing:

> *Be———lay, there! Be———lay!*
> *Ay, ay, be———lay, oh! Be———lay!*
> *Keep us from recks!*
> *Reckless we'll be!*
> *Ay, ay be———lay, oh! Be———lay!*

They sing it twice, thrice, more, whilst there's one at the wheel, each arm bended to it by the bulk of his shoulders. Now and then he'll call to the men, but it's hard to make out all his words as the other men sing on.

'Let go down there! Give them more play! For the love of God, give them more play!'

Mercy me, what a night!—for now it is night. But there's a harsh light on the 'Lady Grace', so that I see all there is to see out there.

I call as well, to the one at the wheel.

'Hey there! Is there something I could do to help?'

I see him take his eyes away from the wheel and look my way.

'No, madam, thank you. Not from where you are! We'll come out of this! You'll see! All we must do is be patient!'

Patient! When you are in a state like this!

Then I think: Could this be the Master? To have such powers of command! The 'Lady Grace' would have to have a master, but could this be *the* Master, the one I have to find?

I have raised my head to call out again with all the powers I have: 'Are you the Master?'

'I have to be right now!' Again he's turned to me. 'No, we lost him before sun up, when we come in to all this. Shame. It would make you weep, if you had time for a tear. He was one you could look up to. But he went over, poor soul.

O'erthrown he was. No-one was there to see him go. We turned, but we could not see him. He must have gone down right away. I was the Two on this show, so it was up to me. But let me see to this!'

He turned the wheel to the right, and then he could speak again.

'We should have come in where you are'—and where's that? I think—'but in all this we cannot. We'll have to keep out here and see if it goes down a little.'

'I wish you well!' I call to him as I go on down again. 'I know you'll make it!'

'Thank you, lady! Could I ask you something?'

'Please do!'

'If you see my daughter, would you say you have seen me? You could say: He will not let you down. Not like last time. He'll be there. Would you do that for me?'

'How will I know your daughter? What does she look like? What do you call this daughter of yours?'

But I cannot see the 'Lady Grace' now, and no answers come.

Q

I have come all the way down, and here's a door, with the words 'The King's Head' over it, and I go in to find young men (as most of them are) in there to make merry.

> *Show me the way to go home,*
> *It's late and I have to go to bed,*
> *I had a little glass, you know, it may be two,*
> *And it's gone right to my head!*

There's a lady with a key in one hand; she would seem to be the head of this commerce. I go over to this lady and say 'Good morning!'

'Here's a good one! She comes in, and what does she say? "Good morning!"'

'Ha, ha, ha!' from most of them there.

She's turned to look at me again.

'Nay, love, it's tomorrow night!'

More 'ha, ha, ha!' from the young men.

I think I should go before this becomes worse, but she's at my arm now.

'It's all right, love. Let's find you a table. Come with me.' She took my hand, and we go over to a table with no-one at it.

By now the young men have gone on to other things.

> On now, Christian soldier:
> Down their stockings falls!
> Take two, have another,
> Fair-faced ladies all!

'This do you?'

'If I'll not be in the way of this lady here...'

'Oh, give no mind to that one. She's well out of it by this time of night. And you know what they say: She's no better than she should be. Now, what would you like?'

'How does he do Cockle-in-Violets?' I ask. 'Dupped, gyved, larded, unbraced...? I could go for something like that!'

'We are right out of it, my love. We'll have more in in the morning, but that's no good, is it? So what would you say to some Long End Fair.'

Long End Fair? What could she have meant?

'Long End Fair: 'are. See? It's the way we speak down here. I could say: I like the look of your hope and grace. Hope and grace: face. You'll see it in no time. If not, I'll coach you.'

'Thank you', I say. But is this where I should be? I do have to have something; that's true. I have had nothing all the time I have been here. But 'Long End Fair'? May be not. Still, should I say no?

'Thank you', I say. 'Indeed, could I please have some of that "Long End Fair", if there's some left?'

'There is. Good, good. Would not have done for me to tell you of it if there had *not* been, would it? And with that?'

'A glass of.... What do you have?'

'We have Cold Countenance; we have White Honey (that's a Flowers); we have Closet Door. That's not all, but the ladies seem to like these.'

'Not imports, are they?'

'No, my love! Naught but good home things here!'

'Then I'll take a glass of White Honey, please.' And I think to ask: 'Will that go well with the Long End Fair, would you say?'

'With the what? La! You had me there! I'll have to keep my eye on this one!'

With that, she left.

> *The maid went over the mountain,*
> *The maid went over the mountain,*
> *The maid went over the mountain,*
> *To see what she could see...*

I had some time, then, to look at where I was. I doubt these young men will know the Master, but may be one of them'll know something—like if it's true you could find a rose that would speak, up by the Well of the Sun. Such a long time's gone by…. How long have I been with O-fie?—when I should have been down here, to do what I have come to do.

Now here she comes again, with the Long End Fair and the White Honey.

'Thank you!' I say. 'That does look good!'

'Given you a little end of good-god as well.'

I look down at what's now on the table.

'Oh! That one's not so hard. Good-god! I love good-god! Thank you!'

'It's been out all day, but I think it'll be all right.'

'Would now be a good time to ask you some things?' I ask.

'Not now, love. And you should give your mind to that, I should think. Not let it go cold. I'll be here again.'

'Oh, before you go, what should I call you?'

'You could call me "Heaven and Hell". See?'

'I *do* see, Heaven and Hell!'

She goes away again, and I have turned to what's before me.

Does not take me long before it's all gone.

Then one of the young men comes over, and he's down on his knees at my table. I truly do not like this. O God, I see he'll sing.

I see the light on the night that I go by
that window,

'Look at you!' Heaven and Hell is here again. 'Now, my love, what was it you had on your mind?'

I see the long-lost remembrance of love
on that door,

'Well, thank you,' I say, 'but what are we to do with, you know, him here?'

She was my lady,

'Let him be; he's like this all the time. But ask away, my love. What's on your mind? I see there's something.'

As she deceived me, I see it, went out of
my mind.

She's bended down so that we may speak.

My, my, my, Rosemary!

'Two things. I have not been here long, so this is still find-your-way time for me.'

By, by, by, Rose—

But he cannot make it to the end before he falls over. One arm's up ... and down again. Then there's no more from him.

'Should we help him up, give him a hand?'

'Better not, love. You never know what they'll do in this state. But what did you say?'

'How I have not been here long. Still have to find my way.'

'Like that for all of us when we come here.'

I let a little time go by, so that she could say more if she would. Then I go on.

'Well, there was a lady—two ladies, I should say, but one of them was the one to tell me—and I remember it well—I should look for a rose that could speak.'

'Where? Did she say?'

'This was when I had been to the Well of the Sun. So it would have to have been close by there, I should think.

'That's some way from here. Not my day-to-day ground at all. Cannot help you there, my love. But *two* things, you did say.'

'I did. You see, I have come here to find another me.'

'Another you! I quite like the one you have!'

'Well, thank you, but the one I have is not right for here. No, that's not it. It's not right for *me*. It was *given* me, in another.... This is all so hard to say. But what I would like to ask you is if you know of the Master—if you know the Master himself.'

'Know what, my love? You think more than's good for you. Now, I should go and call time. But come again another night. We'll have Cold Play here. You know how they'll *never* play now, not in a little how's-your-father like this. But I know how to make men do what I like—what they like, as well. All the way, if you are with me.'

Of that I have no doubt.

> *He'll be knocking up that madam when*
> *he comes,*
> *He'll be knocking up that madam*
> *when he—*

'No more of that, if you please! Time! Time! Out the door, all of you! Take your things and be gone! Time! Time! See you again! Time! Time! Time!'

R

On my way out, when I have almost tumbled on something, my arm's held by one of the young men, and I look at him.

'Thank you!' I say.

'Would you like me to see you home?'

He's a sweet face, and I wish I could take him up on it, but you never know what you'll let yourself in for.

'No thank you', I say. 'Truly.'

There's this as well: I have no home.

But I should say something more, not to let him down more than I have to, so I say: 'And it's still light.'

'When it's not, then.'

Is this a come-on?

'Right. Some other time', I say.

'You let me know. You'll find me in here, like as
not.'

And he's gone.

'Oh, you think so?'

'What?' I look up and down. 'Where are you?'

'Up here, in your head. I did say I would come
with you.'

'And I did say "no".'

'I never take "no" for answers—not from ladies.
And you should think. Down here by yourself?
That will not do, lady, that will not do. You'll
have to have me with you. So here I'll be.'

'And you made your ungracious way in to my
head how?'

'Think I'll let on?'

'I should not ask?'

'And I'll not tell.'

'May be it will be a help to have you with me.'

'Believe me, it will. You'll see. A help in many a
way. Like, would you be up for a go right now?'

'No, I would not!'

'As you like.
      The lady when the light went on
      'Had one hand on his—'

'Will you please not sing!' I say. 'It's more than
I should have to take. You make your way in there
—I cannot tell how—and what do you do? What

all men do when they take their showers!'

'What's that then?'

'If you cannot keep a better tongue in your head—'

'*Your* head, lady. And what would you like me to do with that tongue, whilst here?'

'Keep it still!'

And he does. My expectation went all the other way. And I say nothing, as I take the path away from the 'King's Head'. It's a fair night. I could almost sing, but—could he tell what I think?—he's the one that does, and not as he did before.

Here comes the sun, do–do–do–do,
Here comes the sun, and I say:

'Over to you!'
So I take it up.

It's all right.
Little doublet, it's been a long, cold, wretched
snow time,
Little doublet, in many months it's not
been here.

'You again!'

Here comes the sun, do—be—do—be,
Here comes the sun...

'I could go on like this a good long time', I say.

'So could I.'

And we sing as we go.

'By the way,' I say, 'what should I call you?'

'Robin. That's what they all call me here. Robin.'

'Then I'll call you Robin as well.'.

'And you?'

'O'.

'Good to know you, O!'

'How long have you been here, Robin?'

'Long! I could tell you had things on your mind!'

I'll have to be patient.

'No, but when did you find your way here?' I ask him.

'It's been some time, but not so as to have lost me my youth. That's all I know. And you?'

'Could be it's not been more than a day. May be two. Hard to tell, when the sun would not seem to keep time at all, but rises and goes down as it will.

'I had to come here', I go on. 'I did not know what it would be like.'

'It is what it is.'

'Do you remember not being here?' I ask.

'Remember? Do I know what it is to remember? Do I *remember* what it is to remember?'

'You are all in the now, Robin.'

'I believe so.'

'Wish I could be like that.'

'I like you as you are, O. Let me say this: I love you as you are.'

'I think I could see the Master, when I was up the mountain.'

'You cannot see the Master, O. Did you not know that?'

'How's that? Is he made of glass?' Keep it light.

'No! It's that he's not here.'

'He's not here, but there *is* a Master?'

'There *is* a Master. The one Master. How could there not be a Master, *the* Master?'

'But he's in some other....?'

'That's all I know. He's not here.'

'But I have to find him!' I say.

'O, I have nothing to say. There's no help I have to give you on that one.'

'What do you know of the rose?'

'What?'

'The rose that will speak if you ask it.'

'And if you do not?'

'I have to find that rose', I say.

'There's no more I know.'

'Then I'll be on my way. Thank you for all that you have done for me. So long.'

'But you have to take me with you, O! You'll have to have your Robin!'

S

'Do you know him, O? See him before?'

'Are you still here?'

'Where would you like me to be, O?'

'Up there will do for now, Robin. But him: no, I have not seen him before.'

We have come on some way when these words from Robin make me look to the right to see a steward, as he could be, of some stature. There's something in his right hand, and he'll look down, remember the words, and then look up again, to speak them—to himself as it would seem. But of all this I cannot make out more than a little, here and there.

'...o when will you come to me?...' Nothing before this.

'No, Robin, I have not seen him before. You?''

'...before me, and the shame of my...'

'Does *not* look like one you would find in the King's Head.

'...the memory of them from the...'

'I would not think so, Robin, no. But I'll speak to him.'

'...in thee: let me not be...'

As we come close and see his face, Robin becomes a little jangled:

'Know what, O? I think we should keep away. Let's not be....'

'...all the night make I my...'

'He's all in a night of his own, O!'

'...o Thou, my God...'

'We should not have come over!'

'...For their heart was not right with him...'

'It's all right, Robin. Truly. He's one of these men of God.'

'You think so?'

'...So they shall make their own tongue to...'

'I know so.'

'...I may tell all my...'

'What'll he tell us, O?'

'...And my tongue shall speak of thy...'

'He does not speak to us...'

'...God: God is not in all his thoughts...'

'...but to God.'

'...Many there be which say of my soul, There is

no help for him in God....'

'Would you see if he'll help, O?'

'...help us, o God of...'

'I could ask.'

'...Ask of me, and I shall give...'

'Grave father,' I say to him. 'May I ask you something?'

'...you more and more, you and your...'

'It's this. I have come here in the hope—in the expectation, I would say, I would find another me."

'...another god...'

'I have gone here and there, and have come to believe I would receive help from the Master.'

'...for he shall receive me...'

'But no-one, so it would seem, will tell me where this Master is.'

'...so would we have it: let them not say, We have...'

'If indeed he is here at all.'

'...Indeed speak...

'...in thy light shall we see light...

'...the night shall be light...'

'Oh, Robin! I'll not find this out from *him*!'

'...shall find out all...'

'He'll give no mind to me!'

'...out of mind I...'

'Go on, O! Do not give up now!'
'...up to the heaven, they go down again to the...'
'Do you have the powers to help me here?'
'...him for the help of his...'
'Do you know the Master yourself?'
'...make me to know mine end, and the...'
'If so, what could you tell me?'
'...I would not tell...'
'I have to give up, Robin.'
'...ONE...WITH LIGHT...'
'...OVER...WILL LOOK...'
'No, O! This is to tell us!'
'...OVER WITH...LOVE...'
'Tell us what?'
'...OVER...WILL LOVE...'
'It's like the green light to go, O! Do you see?'
'...OUT...WITH LIGHT...'
'...ONE...WILL LOOK...'

T

If I could have locked his hand in mine I would have done, as we come away and say, the two of us as one: 'Owl!'

'But where to find him?' Thus Robin. 'That mark did not tell us. Down there to the left, do you think?'

'We'll give it a go.'

Away we go, and when that path gives out, we find another.

'You think we should call out "Owl!" as we go?'

'What good would that do? And could you call out from in there? Think.'

'Have you been out to find an owl in the night-time? No? Then please keep the lesson for when you have.'

It's good now to have Robin with me. If we could keep it that way to the time we find the

Master, that'll do for me.

'What was that?'

'Did you see something, Robin?'

'No, but it was like there are eyes on me. Then gone. Then more eyes that look at me.'

'It's nothing', I say. 'It's being out here in the night, when we do not know where we are, where we should go.'

'I know.'

'There, Robin!'

'What?'

'Did you not see him?'

'No.'

And now, as if he answers Robin, comes the call of an owl: 'To-what to-we!'

I look up.

'Do you see him, O?'

'No. There's no light!'

'But he must be up there.'

And the call comes again.

'O owl!' I say. 'Will you tell me where to find the Master, the one I *have* to see, the one I have come here for?'

No call. Nothing.

'It's no good, O.'

'May be not, Robin. Could be this is not the right owl. There must be more than one.'

'Must be.'

'And do we know he meant to say "owl"?'

'You tell me.'

What? This would have made us look at one another—if we could.

'Was that you, Robin?' I ask.

'Not me, no.'

'Then it must have been the owl! He *does* speak!'

'*She* does. Rose the owl here. And what, pray, are you?'

'O', I say. 'You may call me "O", if you would, madam.'

'And me: Robin.'

'Where are *you*?'

Well, this is a hard one to believe, I know, but there's a youth in my head, and now an owl that will speak.

Robin answers: 'In here', but Rose cannot see what he means.

'I do not have to know', Rose goes on. 'I'll say what I have to say to this young lady down there. Now, as you are here, would you like me to sing to you?'

How could I say no?

Rose is quite still. She lets out a little '*do—me— see—me—do.*' Then it's time to sing:

Fair youth, o fair youth,
With flowers on your bed,
But one you have not:
A rose that is sweet.

My love I have lost,
The fair youth did say,
She's gone and away:
Pale owl of the night.

We are being musicked by an owl.

'Thank you!' I say. 'It's not at all what you think it'll be.'

'It's not?'

'I meant, I had not had an owl sing to me before, so I had nothing to go on.'

'I see. It's all in the tongue, you see. But it would take me all night to tell you all the things you would have to remember if you would like to sing as an owl does.'

'I have no doubt.'

'But what have you come here for? Tell me that. Now that you have let me sing to you, you may ask me all you like.'

'Thank you. It's this: I have come here to find another me—'

'Come from when? Come from what?'

What should I say? 'Denmark, then. But I doubt you'll know where Denmark is.'

'Lord, that's rich! You do not know what I know!'

'That's true. Shame on me!'

'Oh, let it go, let it go! Come on, young lady, where do you hope to find this other me, as you call it."

'I believe the Master will give it me; if not, that he'll show me where to find it. And I believe you have access to the Master. Will you please tell me which way to go?'

'You do not go to the Master. He will come to you.'

U

It's hard to tell quite where you are. You may come upon something you think you have seen before, but there'll be a difference. Flowers up in no time; the path falls where before it rose. It's hard, as well—still more so—to tell where you should go.

The Master will come to you, they tell you. Right. How will he find you? Where should you be to make yourself seen? On the grass and not in doors, you would think. But should you go up O-fie's Mountain again?

'What do we do now, O?'

'I do not know, Robin, I do not know.'

'It's time I was home.'

What time would that be, then? What is time here? But it's true that I never did ask him, not from when he dove in to my head the way he did, how long before he would have to go, what he would have to go and do, where his home was, was he on his own. It's been all me, me, me.

All this with the 'rose', the Master.... It's had me on the go all the time. When I was at O-fie's, that was the last time I had a night in bed. You keep on; you never seem to wear yourself out. But we cannot go on like this. Poor Robin!

'Robin, you truly do have the right to go now. It's me to blame, to have had you out so late and so long. It's been good to have you with me, but all good things must come to an end.'

'But look, O, down on the ground there!'

I do look, and see what Robin's seen: a form with words on it.

'Take it up, O, take it up! It may tell you what you have to do so that you'll see the Master!'

I do as he says.

'What is it, O, what is it? Tell me, tell me!'

'Will you please be patient, Robin? I'll tell you, but I have to give it some perusal. Right. This is how it goes:

'"By command of him that could command,

'"Know that we come to you with good will,

'"Know that we see all that you do here, all that you say, all that you speak to, all that you say to them and all that they say to you; all this we know,

'"Know that we know where you go here, up and down, in and out,

'"Know that we see your brother when he comes here,

'"Know that we know of that wretched other brother you have with you right now,"'

'That's me, O. Would have to be me.'

'"Know that we, as well, are with you night and day,

'"Know that we have your good at heart,

'"Know that we see what you do here as noble,

'"Know that we think it would be right to show you mercy,

'"Know that we, like you, do not think that there should be more than one king—in the one state, that is,

'"Know that where you are now—where we are—is a state that is not a state,"'

'Will it go on for long like this, O?'

'Not so long, Robin.'

'Good.'

'Be still now, there's a good Robin.'

'"Know that we do not come to you with sword in hand and do not have to see you on your knees before us,

'"Know that, should you think to do so, we will not let you wed whiles you are here."'

'Will I not have your hand, then, O? Will you not let me make you the Lady Robin?'

'Give over!

'"Know that we love you, as we love no other,

'"This is all we have to say to you,

'"This is all we will say to you,

'"Up to when another day shall come."

'That's the end', I say, 'That's it.'

'So it did not tell you it's from the Master?'

'No, it did not. But *look*: it must be.'

'I would think so. I would take an oath on it.'

'See this here: "By command of him that could command."'

'Must be the Master, then, O.'

'But come to think, there's one way to take that "could", and then there's another way. Could be it means "with the powers to". But could be it means: "had the powers at one time but does not now". Do you see, Robin?'

'Think so.'

'If it's that—"had the powers at one time"— then this would be from the one that *was* the Master and not from the one that *is*, now. And so we would have to look for another Master.'

'*You* would, O. I have to go.'

'I know, Robin. You have been such a help.

What could I give you? What could I say more than "thank you"?'

'That'll do. It was up withered it was. I'll tell them all I had a long, long time in a maid—and then she was not a maid at all.'

'Remember me, Robin.'

'I'll remember you, O. I'll remember you. Out the door and—here I be.'

And there he is.

'Robin—'

'Now you see me—'

And now I do not.

V

And here, in no time at all, is another youth, so that, as I think my hand's touching Robin's, I find it's touching this other one's.

'Thank you for that', comes from him. 'A sweet breath of affection, when I have been here so little time.'

'It was not meant for you', I say.

'But I was the one to take it.'

'What have you come for?'

'What do you think? You turned me on.'

I give nothing away.

'Think that was it?' he goes on. 'Could be.'

Again I say nothing.

'But let's say it was to see you, to be with you. Us two. They all tell me of your beauty, your grace. Such things you have to see for yourself, close up.'

'Now you have seen me. Please go', I say.

'Is that how you think you should speak to me? You do not know what I could be.'

'I do not mind what you are. I know you cannot be the Master.'

'Ha, ha, ha! No, this is not the Master you see here before you. But what if the Master should ask some other to come and see you before he does?—to come and ask you this and that?'

I say nothing.

'What if I should say this to you?' he goes on. '"'Tis in my memory locked."'

At this I find my mind is jangled, worse than in quite some time.

'What are you?' I say.

'No, my sweet. Your words now should be: "And you yourself shall keep the key of it."'

'What are you?' I ask again.

'Come on, you know you have been observed. You have it in your hand, what we left for you, to tell you how things are.'

'I tear it up. Now', I say, and I do so.

'And what do you think that's done for you?'

'I do not know you', I say. 'I have never seen you before.'

'That is true. Here is one not of your cast.'

'Cast?'

'You know what that means. You have not lost all your memory.'

'I ask one more time: What are you?'

'You could call me your Valentine. How would that be?'

'I'll call you Valentine', I say. 'The "my", I think, may be left out. But this still does not tell me what you are, where you have come from, and what made you think you could hope for something from me.'

'Well, my little O, as you call yourself now, it may be that this will help you: "I do not know, my lord, what I should think." Remember that? If not, let me go on: "No, my good lord, but as you did command I did receive his letters."'

'It's not "receive"', I say.

'No? What is it then?'

'"Repel"! "Repel"! As you repel me!'

'There! You see! You *do* remember! "He hath, my lord, of..." But me oh my, I cannot think—'

'Go to hell', I say.

'Now, now, it would be better if we stayed of one mind as we do what we must, would it not? You know how this'll have to go. And it does not have to take such a long time as all that.'

'What does not?' I ask.

'For me to take you with me to where you

should be. You know where that is. Indeed, there's nothing I may say that you do not know before I say it—well before I say it. To give you another take: "My honoured lord, I know right well you did." How does it go then? Remember? "And with them words of so sweet breath...'"

'"...composed..." No! No! No!' I give him one on his wretched face, but he goes on:

'"...As made the things more rich." We may come to an end for now, if you would like. If not, we may go on some more. But it could well be we will not have to. It's all up to you.'

'Do you come from the Master?' I ask.

'That's for me to know and you to find out.'

'I left all that', I say. 'The words you would wish me to remember, the daughter that had to obey, the young soul locked in to something over which she had no command, the love—the love!—that no-one would receive from me: I left all that. I went out in the snow.'

'We *did* see you.'

'I went out in the snow, and I had to choose. It was hard. I will not tell *you* how hard it was. But I went on, and that is how I have come here, away from all that. I had to find—well, I will not go in to that, not if you know it all before I speak'

'It was to look for "another you". I know. We all

know. You did not keep this to yourself, did you? And what did you think this "other you", this "other me", would be like? Tell me! Please! It may be I could help.'

'Go away', I say again.

'That, I fear, I cannot do. Not without you. You would have to come with me.'

'Where?'

'You know where. "Indeed, my lord, you made me believe so."'

'No more!' I say.

'They are all there still. They cannot go on without you. Think how this must be for them: the king and his madam—all right, they may not have been so honorable in what they did to you —*to* you and *with* you—but what of the young lord—you know he had his eye on you—'

I *will* not remember. I *will* not be made to remember by him.

'Will you please take yourself away?' I say.

'—and what of your brother? We could see how it all went when he was here. Touching. How do you think he will have turned out now, when you had him go away?—had him go away without your help and your love?—not to speak of your poor father. Did you never think you should take him with you? You could *do* that if you would give yourself another time there. "Oh, woe is me, to have seen what I have seen, see what I see.'"

I say nothing. I look at him. I keep my eyes on him.

'All right', he goes on. 'Then there's this—I think you'll know where it comes from: "They say a made a good end." Remember? But is it not: "They say *he* made a good end"? Which would you, to give you one of your own words, choose?'

'Not such a difference', I say.

'No, but it is one. You see: you are not one by yourself, my sweet O. There are two of you. May be many more.'

'So are we all. I is a chorus.'

'You think? I have come to restore you to yourself.'

At this there is a shaking, and all falls, is tumbled, blasted, and as if from the ground there comes this long, long sigh: 'Go!'

I cannot see Valentine. He's been blown away.

Words come to me that I do not wish for, but that seem right: 'Gramercy. God b' wi' ye.'

W

Indeed, there's no-one to be seen now, but the words go on that come from down there.

'I had to do that. I hope you are not affrighted.'

'No, not at all. God, how he importuned me! I should thank you. That was all more than I could do with.'

I look down at the grass as I speak, for this—this what?—this profound being cannot be seen.

'That's all right, then. I did think you could take it.'

'It would take more than that to have me in a state by now', I say, and then: 'Could I ask: Are you the Master?'

'Some say so. Not me. I do not.'

'From what I have seen of your powers, you could be, you know', I say.

'Well, thank you, O. May I call you O, by the way?'

'You may indeed. And what should I call you?' I ask.

'Will. "God's Will", some would say. But Will. You may call me Will, O.'

Will did not say he was *not* the Master, so he still could be.

'My expectation, Will,' I say, 'is that you know the reason I have come here.'

'I do. And you think I could help.'

'Well, I do. That's my hope.'

'This "other you", O: do you know what it could be like? Do you know what it is that you have come here to look for?'

'No.'

'Then let me tell you this: there are many things you could be. You could be a young lady in love.'

'I never did know', I say, 'if I *was* in love. As I now see it, I was not, not at all. Not with him, that is. You know, I have done all I could *not* to remember. Now, with you here—well, here and not quite here—I find I may do so, without the fear that memory will rede—'

'Go on, O.'

'—redeliver me to where I was. What is it? Something in how you speak, how your words come with such grace, and honesty—and, I would say, affection. You make me remember my father, and now I do not weep.'

'That is good to know, O. But this "other you": I could make it so that you *are* in love and have no doubt that you are in love.'

'In love with....'

'A youth with sweet eyes and a fair command of words. You would see each other, and that would be it. Head over heels. Joy. Ecstasy.'

'Would I have died by the end?'

'You would.'

I take a breath.

'Would *he?*' I ask.

'He would.'

'Then no, thank you.'

'But you have to think what death is, to such as you—and to such as him. You are not truly dead. You go on and on. I *made* you to go on and on. And you did say this yourself: There is a chorus of you, all over.'

'That's not quite what I meant', I say, but he's on a tear now.

'A chorus of you, and all of you make your way, your own way. You give answers to your brother and your father, and so on. You are a courtier's daughter, and so you have to be there—all of you, have to be—with the king and other observers at the play. You have to be bended out of form by the death of your father. And then you have to—again I say, all of you—do it all again. It goes on and on. There is no true death for you.'

'"Have to", you say. You say it all, with that.'

'There are other things I could make you: a saint; one close to another young lady; one in the clothes of a youth; a king, for you could indeed be a king—'

'You know what?' I say. 'I see this now. It's come to me. This is not the way for me to go on. I have no wish for you to make up "another me" for me. It's not "another me" I have to have; it's the true me. At last.'

'You are right, O. This is hard for me to say, but you are right.'

'I'll be on my way, then', I say. 'But before I go, I think I may have been given a mark, here, over my left eye, from when you rose up from the grave, if that's what you did. Do you have a glass, Will?'

'I may do. I'll look. But remember: You do not face yourself in a glass; you face yourself in yourself.'

Y

With these words of Will's the ground falls away from me. To look at it another way, the all of me rises.

I look at the ground, and there is no ground. I look to the left and to the right, and it's all gone: the mountain path I took on my way here, O-fie's Mountain, the home of the lady of the flowers and that of the two ladies that had to speak over each other, the King's Head—all of it.

I have been raised in to white, almost as it was before.

Have I died and gone to heaven?

There is no fear in me.

There is no expectancy. What will come will come when it will.

Time is still.

You are close to me now. I know you are close to me, which is to say that I know I have come close to you. I was the one that had to make my way. You have stayed where you are, but still been with me as I did so.

This other me: I did not see, could not see, that you would be the one to give me what I most wish for.

There was one lesson I had to give you before this. It was a lesson in how it was for me at home, with my father and brother, and with—but not with—the young lord, and in how I left one day, left it all and went on. On my own.

This now is another lesson, if you like, to make two.

It may be that there will be still another, for this is not the end, by no means the end. I have a long way to go from here.

Come on, you know what we have to do now. You have something I do not have. This is what I ask you now to give me.

Lay your hand on my words. Lay your hand on these words of mine as I speak them. I have come right up here, so close that you must know me to be here from my breath on that hand of yours. In, out; in, out: My breath. I see your hand. Look at it yourself. I have my own hand raised to yours. We are almost touching. It must be now. It must be now. Take that hand of mine and, with all your powers, draw me out.

Acknowledgments

The author remembers with gratitude Harry Mathews, who took an active interest in *let me tell you* and knew how it must start; Lou Rowan, who published two chapters in *Golden Handcuffs Review*; and especially Ken Edwards, who found it a first home in his Reality Street Editions. A revised edition and the sequel, *let me go on*, were first published by Henningham Family Press.

•

The dedicatee of this book knows how much she contributed to it.

There are debts here also to (in order of appearance):

AMIENS (As You Like It)

BIANCA (The Taming of the Shrew)

CALIBAN (The Tempest)

DESDEMONA (Othello)

ENOBARBUS (Antony and Cleopatra)

FOOLS: Fool (King Lear), Feste (Twelfth Night), Elbow (Measure for Measure)

GHOSTS: Old Hamlet (Hamlet), others (Julius Caesar and Richard III)

HERO (Much Ado About Nothing)

IMOGEN (Cymbeline)

JULIET (Romeo and Juliet)

KINGS: Richard II, Henry IV, Henry V, Henry VI, Edward IV, Edward V, Richard III, Henry VII, Henry VIII (history plays)

LAERTES (Hamlet)

MALVOLIO (Twelfth Night)

NURSE (Romeo and Juliet)

OFELIA (Hamlet, Quarto 1)

PERICLES (Pericles, Prince of Tyre)

MISTRESS QUICKLY (Henry IV:1 and 2, Henry V and The Merry Wives of Windsor)

PUCK, or ROBIN GOODFELLOW (A Midsummer Night's Dream)

SHYLOCK (The Merchant of Venice), also the Book of Psalms (King James Version)

TITANIA (A Midsummer Night's Dream)

Uncanonical Text (Sir Thomas More)

VALENTINE (The Two Gentlemen of Verona)